MW01127450

A Journey Most Marvelous

To Lucinda,
Enjoy the ride!
Christine Bradfield

A Journey Must Maintains

A Journey Most Marvelous

Christine Bradfield

Independently Published

A Journey Most Marvelous

Independently published by
Christine Bradfield

ISBN: 9798714484612

Cover design by Christine Bradfield

1.Fiction-Romance-Historical-Victorian. 2.Fiction-Humorous-General.
3.Fiction-Friendship.

facebook.com/authorcbradfield

www.amazon.com/author/christinebradfield

https://books2read.com/ap/nEkwKv/Christine-Bradfield

cbradfield.author@gmail.com

For my lifelong, best friend, Kathy,
the one who really gets me.

You will always be my best audience.

Your laughter and friendship
inspire me like no other.

We are like two peas that fell out of the same
pea holder.

Other Books by the Author

Two Kids and a Notorious Talking Crow

Nonfiction

Millie's Boots

Juvenile Picture Book

From Heart to Hand: Poetry of Life

Collection of Poems

Contents

Chapter 1

I absolutely hated to travel alone. The lengthy, though scenic train ride from Augusta to Raleigh would have been more tedious and tiresome if it had not been for Constance agreeing to make the trip with me. Constance Faith Willoughby, my best friend for most of my adult life, is like ray of sunshine to me. She has fed my heart with laughter and friendship for 50 years now, and for that I feel wonderfully blessed. She laughs, giggles, and sometimes snorts at things I say or do, so of course, that fuels my need to make her laugh. I succeed at it most times. Constance, more than anyone, knows and understands the most about the private side of me. She has accepted all my weaknesses and mistakes, and loved me anyway. She has been a witness to many events in my life. She understands the heartaches I had early on, and why I deeply feel that tomorrows are never promised. She knows those events caused me to make the decision years ago to grab the *tes-ticles* of the bull called, life, and move ahead with determination to enjoy every waking moment on this earth.

Constance and I both share a twisted sense of humor and similar views on life and the world in general. Anything can send us into fits of laughter.

Through the years, it was oft times difficult for others to be around us because we were as silly as schoolgirls when in each other's company. Our youthful energy spilled into pranks, dancing, and other ridiculous shenanigans. I always thought I was a bad influence on Constance, but truth be told, she had a bit of a wild side to her personality, and it popped out sometimes, especially around me. Now that we are older and heading towards our seventies, we are tamer and more subdued, *most* times, that is. Life certainly moves fast, and you are in the ground before you know it, or teetering near the edge like Constance and I. We always chose being ourselves and having fun no matter what others thought. Having Constance with me would make the train trip entertaining and easy, and I was looking forward to having many a laugh and conversation with her during the ride. It had been some time since we had been able to share each other's company for any extended period.

Constance is married to Vernon Willoughby, who is a hard-working man with simple needs and pleasures. Their love and marriage were moving into the fortieth year of celebration. Constance rarely took days away from home, so I felt fortunate that she and Vernon were both so agreeable for her to travel with me for the seven days that I would be on the train and visiting family. Vernon was laconic in nature, but what words he uttered were generally worth hearing. He quietly understood the importance of our friendship, and he never interfered when opportunity gave us the chance to share a lengthy visit. The purpose of my excursion to Raleigh was to attend the graduation of my great niece from the newly established nursing school there, and celebrate the momentous event with my favorite nephew and his family.

Unlike Constance, I, Celia Broadmore, had never married. I was different in that way from most women of my time, not needing a man for security, prestige, or mere survival. I *unquestionably* could have married, and without trying to sound boastful, I did have several offers, yet I chose not to marry. I always felt like a man was more like an *accessory*, or an enjoyment, to be had and savored like the finest chocolate. I never felt a husband necessary to living a full life. It was too restraining and confining for me. I loved variety in all matters of life, you see. My father raised me southern proper and tried many times to marry me off and curtail, what I call my, *zest for life.* Any time he felt I was not behaving appropriately he would always say, "If your mother were alive, this would not be tolerated", while frowning at me in disapproval, as he looked over the top of his eyeglasses. Mother passed before I turned four years old, and daddy was the one who raised me. Other than the hired cook and cleaning lady, I had no womanly influence on me as a small child. From my first breath and first day on this earth, I was a daddy's girl. I most definitely got my way with just about everything I wanted. Daddy was a driven and intelligent man with multiple

3

business ventures. I was left with a very substantial inheritance upon his untimely death that gave me the financial assurance that I could live without a husband, and be an independent woman. I mostly think of myself as an unconventional woman. I have always lived life on my terms, whether it fit with general social practices, or full-out butted heads with them.

I have been privileged to have lived the life I desired. And I have lived without regrets, for the most part, that is. I do not know how anyone can live without some regrets, since we cannot read the minds of others or predict the future. Regret usually occurs more often when we are young, before we know our true selves. Or it arrives after the internal realizations about life and our choices that generally comes in our older years. I think regret is just part of the laws of nature and being alive. I do not dwell on regrets. I have no time and energy for that, and it bears no difference in the outcome. I prefer instead to reflect on the sweetness of the select men I have enjoyed along life's path. All these years I have been fortunate to have stayed independent, happy, and very, *very* content.

As Delby slowed the wagon to a stop near the train depot, my mind abandoned these deeper thoughts and returned to the present. "Oh goodness, we're here!" I announced, unnecessarily. My eyes began searching the milling crowd, and I quickly spotted Constance and Vernon on the platform. I stood in the wagon and hollered,

"Constance! Constance, dear!" I waved my hand in the air, all the while grinning with my mouth wide open. Constance smiled and waved back with less fervor, while Vernon looked like he was struck with a slight pain upon seeing me. Delby busied himself getting my baggage out of the back of the wagon. I gathered my hat and returned it to my head. Then I grabbed my small parcels and waited for Delby.

Delby proceeded around to my side of the wagon and positioned himself to assist me in stepping down from the buckboard. He was close to my age, of average build, and permanently thin, no matter what he ate. However, he was enabled with the unsuspected strength of a younger man. Anytime he assisted me down from the wagon, I always laughed internally, because he took a stance as if he were readying himself for a tug of war. When he offered his hand for support, he also unknowingly contorted his face with the eye closest to me extra wide open. It appeared to me that Delby thought he might die under the abundance of my bosom and my other extra femineity, should I fall on top of him, trying to disembark the wagon. I suppose he was justified, if this was indeed his thought, as I had experienced incidents of pure ungainliness in the past. So far, none of those had involved Delby. He always seemed prepared to defend that record. On this day, I managed to step down without harm to either of us.

"Thank you, Delby. You are a good man. My daddy always said that about your father, and now

I say it about you. You are definitely a fine, hardworking man just like him. I do not know what I would have done all these years without you to help me care for the farm and the house. Do take care of yourself while I'm gone. And Delby, before you go to your cousin's house to help with the new barn, go into the pantry and get a couple of jars of my blackberry preserves to take with you, ya hear."

"That's very kind, Miss Celia. I'll be sure to do that. You do make the darn best preserves! You and Miss Constance have a wonderful trip, now. I will take your luggage on up and have it checked for you. Then I will head on over to pick up the supplies we need, before I go back to the house." I gave Delby a quick, polite hug then turned to make my way onto the platform. I waived my hand in the air again, as I excitedly called out to Constance and Vernon. This time they just stood arm in arm and watched me as I approached, without a wave in reply. I saw Vernon lean to whisper in Constance's ear.

"You know, I think of Celia like a dear friend, just as you, Constance, but her enthusiasm has such volume to it," said Vernon. "Lawdy! She is high energy, that one. And so, so…spirited," Vernon remarked while his brow furrowed.

Constance responded to her husband's comments with a slight grin and a nodding of her head. "That's Celia, alright! I love that she still has the joy of a child in her. She always makes me smile. She embraces the moment and does not

6

care what anyone thinks." Constance folded her arms and watched as Celia weaved through the crowd.

Once we were all together on the train platform, I embraced Constance, and we tried our best to contain our squeals and titters. I did not want to embarrass Vernon in front of the people by acting too puerile. Constance and I looked at each other, and we both had the mutual thought that this was going to be a wonderful trip! We communicated that to each other without words by using a squeeze of our hands, a wink, and our two big grins.

"Vernon, I am most grateful that you can spare Constance to travel with me. It means so much to both of us." I moved to give him a polite hug which he tolerated in his usual stiff-armed manner, while I suspected he was rolling his eyes at Constance over my shoulder.

Constance moved to face her husband. "Vernon, do let the girls cook for you while I'm gone. You are a man of many talents but cooking is not the best of them and you need to eat proper food. Make sure you drink plenty of water when you are out in this heat. And lastly, don't you go forgetting about me while I'm gone," Constance said with a wink, and then she went through the motion of smoothing his lapel.

Vernon leaned in, embraced Constance, and then kissed her gently on the cheek. "And don't you forget how to find your way home, now," Vernon said with a crooked smile. "You ladies have a joyous trip, and I will see you right here in a week from tomorrow." Constance touched his face and smiled at him, and gave him one last hug. The trained whistle blew twice, and the conductor announced, "All aboard!" I grabbed Constance by the hand, and we turned towards the train. "Here we go!" we declared in unison.

On a slightly humid and breezy day in late afternoon, Constance and I waved to Vernon as we climbed the train steps for our adventure. She squealed and danced a little jig down the aisle, excited to be going on the trip, filled with the prospect of seeing new places. We were both eager about having the chance to spend time laughing, talking, and recapturing the feeling like we weren't old at all. Because when we were together, we always felt young, and that feeling often led us to act inappropriately for women of such a mature age. The porter directed us to our seats. Before we allowed our carry-ons to be properly stowed, I retrieved a small bottle of spirits from my bag and discreetly placed in it my purse for almost immediate use. We ladies enjoyed a bit of sippin' now and then, especially when we were together. The whistle blew, and the train chugged out of town. Our laughter was already floating through the train car, causing heads to turn.

It may be hard to believe, but Constance and I could talk non-stop for hours. We even amazed ourselves with that fact on more than one occasion. Our all-time best was thirteen hours straight. We would share discourse about everything from family to world problems. Of course, a large part of every visit entailed reminiscing and recalling times we had shared together during our younger days. Those were priceless and precious memories. That is what you do with best friends when you get older, you sit and talk about the past a great percentage of the time. While Constance was a faithful and loving wife, she did take particular gratification in hearing about my interludes and escapades with the numerous gentlemen, and the occasional scoundrel, that I had entangled myself with during my life. She never judged me or my lifestyle like so many others had done. While I did share many a memorable libidinous moment with her, I was still a most proper southern lady, so the exact details were left to the listener's imagination. Some things should *always* remain private. As the train clacked and swayed into the evening, we began sippin' on our whiskey behind a strategically placed newspaper, and started musing about the days of our past.

Chapter 2

The train would travel through the night and deliver us to Raleigh in the early afternoon on Sunday. As we awoke Sunday morning and prepared ourselves for the day, I could see out the window the occasional church, and sometimes hear their distant bells ringing to gather their congregation. This caused me to stop and contemplate and share my thoughts with Constance.

"You know, I accept that there is a place in this world for religion and faith. People need something to believe in to give them hope in harsh or threatening times. I suppose they need to be able to express gratitude to an Almighty when they are blessed with good fortune or saving grace. I think for most believers, religion provides them with guidance in their everyday living to help them to try to stay on the straight and narrow. I do conclude that there is higher power, but I never truly felt the call to attend church services, although, my father certainly thought I should. Confining me to a space at designated times to sing and say *amen* could not possibly be the one thing to save my soul."

Constance chuckled and shook her head at my statements as she put on her stockings and shoes.

"I always felt being kind and generous and living the golden rule would rescue me from the fires of hell."

"The fires of hell are already lapping at your skirt hem, Celia. Unless you change soon it is going to be too late for salvation. Is your sermon about over? I'm hungry."

Then a thought struck me awfully funny, and I let go of a big laugh. Constance began to laugh too at the sight of me being so tickled by my thoughts.

"What is so darn funny, Celia! I'm laughing at you laughing, and I don't even know why I'm laughing."

As I gasped for breath I said, "I was thinking about the times in my life I had specifically spoke out loud the Lord's name. I was recalling numerous times when I had been so near *heaven,* and yet had never left my boudoir. I must say that in many an interlude with a chosen male companion, I have experienced spectacular episodes of pure joy, and often called out the name of the Lord to express the gratitude for the moment. I certainly feel that I have been endowed with great favor to be able to experience such gratifying carnal exchanges of reciprocity. I fear many women do not or cannot enjoy the pleasures of unbridled intimacy for a variety of reasons. One thing is for sure, I am a faithful member of that bedroom congregation, and I attend *services* as often as I can manage. Praise the Lord! Then show the man the door, please."

"Celia! Oh girl! You are so bad! And talking that way on the Sabbath! Mercy me!" My irreverence did not stop Constance from laughing though; it never did. I am sure they heard our cackling in the rooms next to us. Constance laughed so hard at my remarks that she spit and sputtered and found it hard to breathe. She fell to the bed holding her belly, because it hurt so much. She pleaded with me to stop talking in such a manner.

Constance let out an exhausted sigh once she stopped laughing. "There is no way you will escape Hell's fires because of the extraordinary amount of *zest* you have been born with, and cannot keep contained. The devil has had you on his list for some time now, Celia."

I acted as if to swat at her. "Come on, Miss Constance, let's go to the dining car for breakfast and have us something special. It is Sunday after all, and we have been talking an awful such. I hope we don't burst into flames."

Constance adjusted her hat in the mirror, turned towards me, and placed her hands on her hips. "Well, I have already had words with the Lord about you. I asked him to be careful of his aim when he sets you on fire and not to strike me too. I told him that I am a poor soul who took mercy on you, so you will have at least one friend in this world."

"Oh, poor you! The bull crap is flying early today! Now what sounds good for breakfast?"

We had a surprising lovely breakfast. We thoroughly enjoyed our window views of North Carolina amid the exchanges of pleasantries with those seated near us. We discovered an older couple who were from the same town in Ohio where Constance grew up, and several people who were also traveling to Raleigh. One young woman droned on in talk about her children. I nodded occasionally, as if I cared what she had to say, until she finished eating and left the car. Constance proceeded to talk about the tribulations of her grandson since the mysterious departure of his wife, and while I was interested and listened attentively, when the door of the dining car opened, and I glanced to see who was coming in, I went deaf to all the rest of the words Constance uttered. I realized my cheeks were suddenly burning hot, and my heart had begun to pound with excitement.

I could not believe he was standing there. Colonel Parker Boyd, right here, right now. If you had smacked me in the face with a dead fish at the very moment, I doubt I would have felt it. I was *unbelievably* at a loss for words, and I quickly turned to fidget with my purse to avoid eye contact with him. I promptly realized Constance was trying to get my attention and was saying my name out loud. I looked up at her, and then at Parker. I had no choice but to meet this situation head on.

When Parker heard my name, his head turned towards our table. He looked at us, then only at me, as if to verify to himself if this was *his* Celia. He turned back, paused a moment, and then walked over to our table. To see him this way, without warning, I thought I might pee my britches. He was one of two men in my life that I truly had loved, and

14

admittedly, one of two that I had considered marrying. He left Augusta most expediently once I had declined his marriage proposal, and that was the last I had seen or heard of him, until now. He had no idea my heart and all my love were in his pocket that day when he left. Now here he stood in front of me. Of course, he no longer wore a uniform, but he still had an air of command and capability about him. His age showed a bit in his grayed hair, and the crow's feet around his eyes, yet he was still a striking man. He was strong and fit in stature, and more handsome than ever. As I looked at him, I was melting like ice cream in August. I took a deep breath, swallowed, and strained to gather myself into coherence in order to speak. Thank goodness he spoke first.

"Celia Broadmore! I cannot believe my eyes," he said in his syrupy, deep, southern voice, as he gently took my hand and kissed it.

"My goodness! Parker, hel-hello. This certainly is an unexpected meeting," was all I could manage to say without spitting and choking.

Parker was the type of gentleman that any woman would want. He was so completely proper and charming as hell. He had a talent of making a woman feel as if she was the only woman in the world that deserved his attention. You could have missing teeth and pimples, be covered in mud, and if Parker talked to you, you instantly felt like a natural beauty. He was a genuine and unselfish man, and that was rare. I was in shock and disbelief that he was here in front of me after all this time. I was more shocked at the sudden feeling like he had never left. It was almost as if my feelings for him had been asleep all these years, and they had now decided to stir and be recognized.

He turned and greeted Constance, and then he turned to me again. "Since I am traveling alone, may I please share the table with you ladies?"

Before I replied, he had moved into the seat next to Constance, directly across from me. His dark brown eyes still deep and consuming, just like I remembered. He smiled, and that was all it took. I was transported right back to the night we met at the mayor's home with the two of us standing on the balcony at sunset. Old as I was, I felt like I was being hit with love for the first time. I was melting quickly. Drippin'...drippin'...drippin' to the floor to be wiped up later with an old cleaning rag. Trouble was coming. No, trouble was sitting at the table with us. Lord! Lord! Lord! Please give me strength! Like most heathens, I would suddenly become religious when found in a position of needing divine intervention and rescue. While I had planned on reminiscing about some of my love life with Constance, as she had requested, I surely did not expect to meet any of them face to face again, especially not Parker.

I caught sight of Constance whose eyes were moving rapidly back and forth at each of us, similar to someone watching a tennis tournament. She was squirmy in her seat too. I could see her tension in the tightness in which she held her lips. She knew what I had felt for Parker, so she probably suspected what was going on my mind as the three of us began polite chatter. The porter interrupted our conversation shortly after it began to announce that in ten minutes the train would be stopping in Charlotte to drop off and take on new passengers, as well as to resupply the fuel and water.

Parker frowned after hearing the announcement. He then stood and buttoned his topcoat. "Celia, Constance, it has been an extremely wonderful surprise and a sincere pleasure, but that is my cue to leave. I must get off the train in Charlotte. I cannot believe that we met like this, and so quickly I must leave you. There is so much more I wish to talk to you about. If only we had more time right now."

Hallelujah! I thought to myself. Divine intervention had arrived and on time! I would be saved from making a fool of myself. I was unnerved by my overwhelming desire for him to stay. I was already seeing a glimmer of a second chance in my mind.

As he bid us goodbye, he took my hand, but instead of kissing it, he leaned in and kissed my cheek, and whispered to me. "Celia, I believe fate has decided we should have another chance. You *will* be hearing from me. I don't believe this is another goodbye." And with that said, he stood tall, smiled that gorgeous smile of his, turned and left the train car. We sat there dumbfounded with our mouths agape.

Constance kicked me under the table, and I stifled a squeal. As soon as the door clicked shut behind him, Constance and I let out a whoop and a holler, jumped up, grabbed each other, and spun in circles. We were beside ourselves with what had just occurred. Others in the dining car watched us in amazement and curiosity, as if we old ladies were a side show at the circus.

"Can I get a hallelujah?" I shouted.

"Can I get an Amen?" Constance chimed.

After a few moments of happy relief, I directed Constance to run quickly to our private compartment, so that we might get a glimpse of Parker as he exited the train. We scurried back to our compartment, like mice running for a hole in the wall, squealing and laughing in a very unladylike manner. Both of us almost fell down on the way when my shoe fell off, and I stumbled into Constance. Once inside the car, I pulled back the curtain, and I pushed Constance close to the window to be my eyes.

"Oh, Constance! Let me know if you see him. I cannot appear too eager. I do not want Parker to see me looking for him." I fanned myself to cool down and paced within the small space.

She squealed a little and said in a slightly breathless and rushed voice, talking louder and louder as she spoke, "Celia, I can't believe this happened! Parker, here with us! With you! Divine intervention, hell! This is a damn miracle, girl!" She had said this so loudly I thought everyone on the train would hear it. We both giggled nervously like schoolgirls.

She quickly turned back to the window to focus on the passengers leaving the train. Then she yelled. "There he is, Celia! There he is!" pointing as she hollered. I leaned over her shoulder to look, and suddenly he was right there near our window looking at us both. I knew how smart Parker was, and he had no doubt found out through some method which sleeping car was ours. He tipped his hat to us. I moved closer to give a short wave. He stared at me purposely and intently as he raised his right hand, then he tapped lightly two times on his chest where is heart was, and left his hand to rest there. Then he shot me his notorious, killer grin, turned, and melded into the crowd, and away.

Once he was gone, we made high-pitched squeals and hooted. We fell onto our beds as if we had a case of the vapors. We laughed it up for several minutes before regaining our composure. We were two gray-haired, old ladies acting as if we were young girls sharing secrets of a first romance, spread eagle on the beds, wearing old lady shoes and saggy stockings.

"Celia, you must be the luckiest woman on earth to have a man like that come waltzing back into your life. Or you must have one heck of a guardian angel! Wait until I tell Vernon about this! I am sure he will exercise a plethora of words concerning this

19

surprising turn of events!" We laughed out loud, again.

As we lay there catching our breath, I thought to myself, Celia, why, oh why, did you let him leave years ago? That man is like a mouthful of cinnamon and sugar, the excitement of a Christmas morning, and the beautiful explosions on a July fourth, all wrapped in the most handsome of male packages. What on *earth* were you thinking back then? With the clarity of hindsight, I realized that I must have been a half-wit with temporary insanity, or perhaps I experienced an unexplainable neurological glitch in my thought process. This surprise of seeing Parker today was taking me to giddy heights, just like when I first met him. Was I really going to get a second chance with him? It was almost too much to think about.

Chapter 3

As our blood pressure returned to normal, after the second coming of the Colonel, I tried to tell myself to push the thoughts of him to the back of my mind. I could not let thoughts of what ifs, what could be, what had been, and such, take over my brain. So, after making a few pertinent notes in my private journal, I closed it and put it away. I leaned my head back on the seat and tried thinking of other things besides Parker. I looked over at Constance. She had an amused look on her face, as if she might be thinking about the morning's events.

Constance looked up from her needlepoint and said, "Celia, what are you going to do about Parker?"

"Ab-so-lute-ly nothing at this point in time. I have no way to predict the future, and I am not going to worry myself with that now. I learned long ago that life, if ever, rarely turns out like we plan, or matches our hopes. Better to roll with circumstances as they happen, and let worry and fret find a home somewhere else."

"Yes, I think you are definitely right about that," Constance agreed. She nodded in understanding while still looking down at her needlepoint.

As I sat with my eyes shut trying to calm myself, Prudence Smythe suddenly popped into my head. Why would Prudence suddenly come to mind after being all riled up about Parker? I realized I had never shared with Constance what Prudence felt that she needed to share with me the last time I ran into Prudence. For all my life, and always out of the blue, people I did not know or barely knew, have chosen to share details of their life with me, sometimes very *personal* details. It was a curse I believed I was born with, and one I carried all my days. I began to tell Constance about what had happened when I bumped into Prudence a few weeks ago, and how I was put in a position of edification.

Prudence was a woman we both only casually knew. She had come to the Augusta area with her fiancé, Elmer Smythe, a few days prior to their marriage. He had met her in Savannah while there on business, and in matter of a week, decided that she would be his wife and proposed to her. He brought her back to Augusta for the marriage. I had been introduced to Prudence at a social gathering at the home of Elmer's sister to introduce Prudence to a few members of the community. I was as polite as I could be as she seemed most interested in talking to me more than some of the others in attendance. Her conversation was more than uninspiring. I finally pushed her in the direction of the pastor, and I made my polite exit out the door, before the woman had a chance to latch onto me again.

If you knew what Prudence looked like, you would understand that she was *extremely* fortunate to have had even a single proposal come her way. I know it is not proper, and another reason I shall not escape damnation, but I called her possum-face Prudence.

"I forgot to tell you about seeing possum-face a few weeks ago." Constance laughed as I said the nickname out loud.

"Do you remember how Prudence holds her mouth in the puckered up, O-shape? You know, it reminds me of an asshole on a cat," I said. We both busted out laughing.

"I surely do. And you are right. It does look like a cat's ass. You talk so *awful,* but you sure make me laugh so much. I will probably face damnation myself for laughing at all the terrible things you say."

I began to tell Constance about how I recently found out something very unnerving and quite shocking about Mr. Smythe. I explained about my encounter with Prudence, and a burden that she felt necessary to share with someone. Unfortunately, I turned out to be the surprised receiver of such.

It was just a few days after she had married Elmer, when I spied Prudence in the clothing store. That possum face of hers was peering through the racks and shelves, but not really seeming to be looking at all. She had an extra stressed appearance to her already odd face. As she approached me, I said a courteous hello to her. Then unknowingly, I made the mistake of also asking how she was doing.

"Oh, I'm fine," she replied. Then she paused and looked down as she wrung her hands together and fussed with the cuffs of her sleeves. It was clear by her face and her actions that something was wrong. Goodness me, sometimes I hated that I felt the need to care about others, because it frequently put me in awkward and uncomfortable situations. I also never knew when to keep my mouth shut. I knew as soon as I said it, I would regret it.

"Prudence, there is clearly something troubling you. Is there anything I can help with?"

She looked down at the floor, then tilted her head slightly sideways to look at me, and said, "Celia, do you mind if we sit and talk for a minute? I need to share something with another woman, and you are the closest thing to a friend I have here in this town." Once again, feeling regret coming at me full speed, I agreed. We went outside and sat on the bench in front of the store.

"Go ahead, Prudence, tell me what is wrong." I bit my lip in an anticipation of what was coming.

Prudence began to speak stating that what she had to say was an extremely delicate matter to discuss, and that she needed my assurance that it would go no further than our conversation. I gave her the confidence that I would keep my word of privacy, and she continued. She spoke in a quiet and nervous voice.

"You know, I am an educated woman who has been schooled in biology and other subjects. I had a pretty good idea of what to expect on my wedding night, because I had witnessed nature's actions with livestock on our farm. But Celia, nothing prepared me for what I saw when it came time for Mr. Smythe and I to consummate our marriage."

Oh lord! Oh lord! I screamed in my head. I tried not to let my eyebrows shoot up. I could not believe the subject she was about to share with me, and the boldness of how she immediately got to the point of her vexation. I grabbed onto the arm of the bench and could not wait to hear more!

She fidgeted a bit and then proceeded. She said when Mr. Smythe had undressed, and she was able to see his *maleness,* that she had to stifle a scream. She thought of bolting out of the room, but her feet felt as if in cement, due to the shock of what she was seeing. She spoke even lower now and leaned in to whisper to me.

"He was so *large*, so *horse-like*," she whispered. As she told me this, it was hard for me to picture the small frame of Mr. Smythe with such a large appendage. I feared he must have looked like he had a third leg. I suddenly had a flash of memory about the rumor I heard years before about Mr. Smythe's granddaddy. It was said that he had been turned away from the local brothel because none of the *ladies* employed there could *handle* him.

25

Apparently, Elmer had inherited the best of his granddaddy's genes!

After hearing Prudence's last statement, I had to contain my laughter and maintain a somber face, and that surely was not an easy task. She continued to talk and said that she was extremely scared about *accommodating* him, but knew what was expected of her as his wife. Still speaking in a whispered voice, she told me that after a few minutes of amorous activity, the moment came when she was *introduced* to his male member. With that statement, she looked away for a moment and paused, twisting her hands around and around as she sat. I was not sure what I should do to comfort her. I just sat there, almost frozen, waiting to hear more.

After a few moments, and with regained composure, she said *the act* had been over quickly, but not without an extreme amount of discomfort and pain on her part. She fretted about how she could continue to be his wife in this manner for fear he would, and in her words, *tear her up,* and that she might not walk right, *ever.* Seeing the look on her face, I thought she was going to cry. I grabbed her hand and tried to assure her it would be alright before long, and to give it some time. However, what I did not tell her is that previously in my life, I had also found myself in the company of a man who had the same *condition.* I certainly had not found that to be a problem at all. I thought of it more like a ticket to *heaven*, you might say. Instead, I told her that compromises could be made, and to be honest with Mr. Smythe, because he clearly loved her, and together they could work things out. Prudence seemed to believe my words. She left after thanking me for being a friend and listening to her concerns.

After Prudence left, I sat there and pondered what I had just learned. Then it struck me. And it struck me hard and funny. I bent over with laughter until I had tears in my eyes. People passing and seeing me like this were surely judging my mental state. My uncontrolled laughter stemmed from having the revelation of now knowing why Prudence had that cat-assed, O-shaped, puckered-up mouth on her face. It was all Mr. Smythe's fault!

Constance was laughing so hard now that she almost fell off her seat. We both laughed until our bellies hurt and tears welled in our eyes.

"Celia!" Constance barked, "you are going to turn to stone for thoughts like that. I don't know why I even associate with you."

Of course, we both knew why she did. We were same of heart and thought. It was just that I was the one who was always bold enough to say things out loud and with a bit more embellishment. It was at this moment that I realized why my brain had made the connection between thinking about Parker, and suddenly having thoughts of Prudence and her predicament. And with that thought a big, pleased smile came across my face, and my eyes smiled too.

Christine Bradfield

Chapter 4

We were jolted back to the present moment with the train whistle blowing, and the announcement by the porter that there would be a short stop in Greensboro to pick up and drop off passengers. When the train had fully stopped, Constance and I decided to stand and stretch our legs. We watched to see who got on or off the train. In our minds, we were not nosey old ladies, we just liked being informed. Several men in suits waited for a young woman to board the train. She had twin boys in tow. The twins were adorably cute. They were dressed alike in pale blue outfits. They seemed to be a little feisty and hard to hold onto, as she guided them up the steps of the train car.

"Oh Constance, seeing those twin boys makes me recall those irresistible Conrad brothers," I said with a devilish grin.

"You haven't mentioned them in years. I remember how your daddy disliked those boys."

"You're right. That was certainly a *long* time ago. I do not believe old age and infirmity will ever dislodge those handsome boys from my memory." I breathed a deep sigh and smiled, and went floating back in time in my mind.

"Celia!" Constance snapped. "Go on now and tell that story. I only vaguely remember the details. Tell me again what happened with those brothers. I do remember it being a real doozy of a situation, though." She smiled at me. Her eyes twinkled with anticipation.

"Oh, all right, but once I tell you realize your ears cannot *unhear* it. Hold on to your seat, little lady." Constance adjusted how she sat in her seat as if preparing for a photograph. She folded her arms and then nodded to me to indicate she was ready for me to proceed.

I began to ruminate all the way back to when I was sixteen years old. That was the year I became debutante, and I attended my first and only cotillion ball. I had been away at finishing school, and I had only recently returned home. That was the night I met the Conrad twins. At eighteen years old, they had moved to Augusta the month before with their family, and I did not know much about them. What was obvious was that they were deadly handsome. They each sported a charismatic smile that would make any lady want to drop her bloomers. It was on this night that I was being *presented*, with my father's blessing, to a select group of potential suitors who had been invited to the ball. It was held at the Waterman's home outside of town, just past the church. Daddy gave me a gift of a necklace with a small gold cross that night. I truly think he thought it would save me from myself by hopefully discouraging my *zest*, or at least decreasing it somehow.

Cotillion was usually for those between the ages of sixteen to eighteen, boys and girls. For girls, if you were not engaged or married by eighteen, you were probably doomed to a life as a spinster. Although I was just sixteen, I was not as *delicate* as most young ladies at that age. Being shown off to potential, well-bred young gentlemen for the possibility of marriage made me feel like a hog at auction. I only did it to please my daddy and not embarrass him in front of the other Augusta society members. He was a man of prominence in our town. Since he had sole responsibility for my upbringing, he would dutifully make sure that his daughter, however stubborn and independent, would be schooled in good manners, ballroom dance, and other genteel behavior. He foolishly thought that after proper *lady* instruction, that I might be persuaded to change my ideas on marriage. But it didn't work. I definitely did not want to attend the night's event, but I could always make the best of any situation. I managed to enjoy myself with the *strategic* use of my dance card. And I had those Conrad twins in my line of fire as soon as they arrived at the doorway of the ballroom. I could hardly take my eyes off them. If I had to be at this cotillion ball, it was going to be on *my* terms.

Several of the young men asked to dance with me, including Jent Whidbey. Daddy thought he was high quality because of his rich parents and supposed intelligence. I thought he was too full of himself. In my opinion, his face gave no suggestion of intelligence at all, and when he spoke, he confirmed that assumption. I had absolutely no interest in him. I creatively steered him in the direction of the mousey, Miss Linnie Wilson. Linnie would listen to his arrogant talk all night and drink it in like water. When I took a sideways glance at them moments later, I saw my tactical move was already working. Linnie's face appeared as if she was cherishing every word he uttered in her direction.

Tonight, I politely declined all but the Conrad brothers when it came to adding names to my dance card. When those boys were side by side, the only way to tell them apart was that Jared was a wee bit taller than William. As we talked, even their voices were so similar that I felt like I had double vision while they both stood in front of me. While I fended off the glances of other debutantes by placing myself to block their view of the brothers, I worked my *flirtatious* talents on them. Both boys seemed very agreeable to dancing with only with me, and they took turns filling my dance card for the entire evening. They were adept at dancing, and I felt like a butterfly moving from one flower to the next, switching back and forth between them. I soon realized through individual conversations that Jared and William were very competitive. Each waited impatiently for their next turn to dance with me or bring me refreshment. I found each one delightful, charming, and *irresistible*. There was no doubt, even from the first moment, that I was enamored by each brother. It was like I had no control of what was happening in my brain. I felt trouble coming... double the trouble, that is.

The twins were saturated with masculinity and virility. I wanted *both* pieces of candy. My damnation would be signed and sealed if I dared enjoy both these fine chocolates. I couldn't possibly...well, maybe. Oh, hell yes, I was going to try. First though, I had to figure out how to tell them apart when they were not together, because both Jared and William detested being taken for the other brother. I dared not make that mistake. I doubted that I could call either Sugar or Darlin' for very long before I would be found out. On this night, my dance card allowed me to keep them straight. What I needed was a sure-fire way to distinguish the two, should I run into one or the other in town, or elsewhere. Tonight, I decided I would just relish being a hummingbird, enjoying the nectar of each flower, as we danced through the evening.

My father noticed how I was solely dancing and talking with only the Conrad boys. He passed me in the hall on my way to the powder room, and he reminded me that I was here to mix and mingle with all those in attendance.

"Celia, do not limit your options, honey. Please move about and let everyone get to know you and see how smart and delightful you are." He said this with a calm but firm tone in his voice. It was the tone

33

that he used when he wanted to be sure you were paying attention to his words.

I smiled a sweet smile at him and said, "Yes, of course, Daddy. I will do that," and gave him a quick hug and went on my way.

I already knew that I would only partially comply with Daddy's request in order to appease him. I had to stay focused on my plan to block the other debutantes from the brothers, while I simultaneously and politely avoided any other suitors. All this maneuvering was going to be exhausting, but it would be so worth the end result, if my plan worked.

Now back on the dance floor, it was time to take further action. I decided I would prey on the lack of confidence and the abundance of self-consciousness of the young, want-to-be-engaged females. I pulled out my handkerchief and dabbed at the sweat on my brow and gathered myself for the first part of my plan. The too sweet and too pretty Aubriella was my initial target. Before moving next to her, I needed to pass by the dessert table first.

"Hello, Aubriella. You look very beautiful in that dress. Spin around and let me have a look, will you."

"Thank you, Celia. My mother insisted my father buy this dress. It was *very* expensive. I just love the style and all the layers." Aubriella pulled at the sides of her skirt to fan out the material, and began to twirl around. I feigned a loud gasp when her back was to me. She stopped and turned to look at me again. Her brow was wrinkled with concern.

"Quick, come with me! I have to tell you something," I said. Then I grabbed her elbow and pulled her over near the wall.

"What is it, Celia? Why did you gasp? Is something wrong with my dress?"

I leaned in close to Aubriella and whispered. "You may want to go and check the back of your dress. Um...well...there is *something* on it."

"Something on my white dress? Oh god! What is it?" Her eyes widened with fear.

"Goodness, me," I said with a sigh, and then paused for dramatic effect, as I looked at the floor. I raised my head and looked her straight in the eye. "Sugar, I fear you may be having your *monthly* visitor."

She covered a scream with her hand and ran. If I was lucky, she would run all the way home before finding out it was cherry pie that I had smeared on her dress, which I had concealed in my handkerchief.

I then proceeded to go greet and talk with Lucille Beddows. I secretly called her Lucille Brussel Sprouts. She was someone who I really disliked and found hard to stomach. I thought she always acted as if she were better than me, or anyone else for that matter. She bullied anyone that allowed it. I sashayed up behind her and then stepped to the side of her. Hoping the noise would cause her to turn in my direction, I snapped open my fan.

35

"Miss Lucille, are you enjoying the evening? Do you have a full dance card?"

"I would enjoy it more if you would let loose of those Conrad twins. Do you really have to keep dancing with both of them? It is not very *ladylike*. Besides, I heard your daddy tell you to mingle."

"Miss Lucille, all you have to do is smile the gorgeous smile of yours, and those boys will forget me and run right over to you," I said with the sweetness of syrup dripping from my words. She was so full of herself that I knew if I said this she would immediately start smiling. And like a puppet, she did just that. She smiled big and looked around the room as if she was searching for the twins, radiating confidence, as if she was the queen of England.

"Oh dear! Oh goodness!" I said as I raised my fan to shield my eyes. I pretended as if I did not want to look directly at her, as if something were wrong with her face.

"Celia, what is your problem? What is *wrong* with you?"

I stepped closer to Lucille and lowered my voice while still shielding my face somewhat with my fan. "You have some food stuck between your front teeth." I embellished the lie by adding a grimace to my face as I spoke. She let out a faint squeal, covered her mouth, and then ran down the hall as if her skirts were on fire. The sight of this made me giggle. How easy this was turning out to be.

As I looked back at the gathering, I noticed Cynthia Bullard walking straightway in the direction of the twins, but I beat her to the destination. I sensed the determination of this biddy chicken by her movements, and saw her flash a look of disdain in my direction. She had no idea who she was dealing with; I was not going to share *my* chocolates. This would not do. After maneuvering to get next to her, then making a bit of polite small talk, I made a move as if I were turning to step away. I *accidentally* stepped on the hem of Cynthia's skirt, ripping it slightly. The move also caused a tear at the waistline seam.

"Oh, my goodness, I am so very sorry, Cynthia. I am so clumsy sometimes," I said with all the sincerity I could muster in my voice. "Let me help you, dear."

"Oh no!" she growled through gritted teeth, as she checked the damage to her dress. The fiery glare in her eyes sliced off my head. "Celia, you have elephant feet and there is not an ounce of grace in your body!" She continued to inspect the damage as she huffed.

Instead of helping her in her dilemma, I waved and called to Beth Ann and asked her to help Cynthia. Beth Ann was on the *slow* side of normal thought, you see, so I knew she would help without questioning my request. And she did. And that took care of getting Cynthia away from the Conrads, at least for the time being.

It was then I had a thought of moving the three of us outside to the garden to get away from most of the guests. That would make it less exhausting for me, I thought, less bullets to dodge, you might say. I smiled to myself, because I somehow understood, even as a very young girl, how easily men could be led and manipulated by a woman. Men were as eager to please as children and just as clueless, so easily pulled along. All it took was a whiff of femininity, and they were putty. With that idea, I looped my arms through theirs and easily guided the twins through the room, out the brilliant glass doors leading to the veranda, and down the wide stone steps that met the garden path.

The evening was close to perfect. The sun was almost below the horizon in a gorgeous display of deep oranges and yellows. It would soon be dark. The moon was already out. A light breeze kept us cool even in our fancy clothes. After a short stroll, we found ourselves standing by the backyard pond. Beautiful water lilies added to the reflection of the moon on the water. The fragrance of magnolia blossoms floated on each gentle breeze. There was a bench nearby, and Jared suggested we sit for a spell. Working on my hastily preconceived plan, I pretended to feel parched and asked if Jared might get me a drink. And with haste, he left to do so. I simply wanted a few minutes alone with William. I hoped I could work my womanly magic on him first.

I pretended to shiver and say I was feeling chilly. William, in true gentlemanly fashion, promptly took of his jacket, leaned into my direction, and placed it around my shoulders. As he leaned so near to me, I thought what a *wonderful smell* he has about him. It was a manly smell, but not offensive. Seductive? Yes, seductive, that was it. I had never experienced the laws of nature and attraction in this way before. The discovery flustered me. How could the scent of someone have such power? I managed to tilt my head slightly in order to smell the jacket collar after he had placed in on my shoulders. I was suddenly feeling very *stirred up* by him. With this new revelation, I thought William must be my choice. I will be able to choose only one of the brothers, and hopefully, I will not live an eternity in Hell. As I began to fantasize about what it would be like to have William kiss me, Jared appeared by my side on the bench, sweet tea in hand, and jarred my romantic thoughts of William to a complete halt.

"Thank you, darling. This is just what I needed." I took a sip and smiled and patted him on his knee. He grinned wide and winked at me. I guess neither brother realized I had already drunk a bucket of tea this evening. They had competed all night to bring me refreshments and dote on me.

The conversation changed to how the local crops were faring without enough rain, to the church social coming up next week, and then other pleasantries. It was then that the boys' father stepped outside and called William to come inside. His father said he wanted to introduce him to the local banker, Mr. Watkins, and discuss the business venture William had suggested to his father. I handed him his jacket with a thank you. I said that he needed it to meet the banker in order to be presentable. He nodded and smiled. He grabbed his jacket and returned to the house.

Divine intervention had arrived quickly this time, even without my sinner's plea. William's departure had allowed me a few private minutes with Jared. I could not help but wonder if Jared had his own smell, and would I find it as arousing as William's. My devious mind churned on how to quickly get close to Jared before William returned.

"Jared, my dear, turn around, please. I do believe you have a leaf or bug in your hair. Let me get it for you."

With that request, I stood and walked behind the bench, claiming I could see it better that way. While pretending to try to get it something out of his gloriously, thick and wavy black hair, I leaned in and breathed deeply. My ankles went weak. Lord a'mighty! He too had a most delicious smell. What special ingredient had these boys been made with that would make a gal feel this way? Whatever it was, it was magical and most intoxicating to me. I wanted to nibble at him right then and there. Instead, I rose back up, and when I did, there stood William. I almost let out a noise at being startled. The surprise of William sent my sensual thoughts of Jared rushing out of my mind at full speed.

"There, there, I got that darn bug out of your hair," I said, as I brushed the shoulders of Jared's jacket, acting as if I was cleaning the bug off of his coat.

I quickly regained my composure and got my body temperature back to normal best that I could. I suggested to the brothers that we go back inside and enjoy more of the music. I secretly feared Daddy would come looking for me if I stayed outside too long. Locked arm in arm, we slowly sauntered back to the house. After what just happened in the garden, I knew how I would always be able to tell the brothers apart. I also knew at that moment there was no way I could only have one chocolate; no way in hell. And Hell would surely be my destination when all was said and done. What I had not yet realized, however, was how intertwined the three of us would continue to be in the weeks to come.

The rest of that sweet spring turned out to be a remarkable and most memorable one. The Conrad brothers and I became inseparable. I know I surely gave my father fits of worry and sleepless nights during those months. But after weeks of our *togetherness*, both brothers were sent off to college in Boston, and we never saw each other again. We shared a few letters, but the brothers focused their energy on education, and after that, on starting a successful business together. I assume that I slowly faded from their minds. The three of us had a unique and special relationship. One I could have *never, ever* have imagined before the night we met.

41

As I prepared to finish telling the story, I saw that Constance held her needlework tight in her hands. She had listened intently to everything I said. Her lips were tightly pursed in anticipation of what might come next.

"Constance, let's just say that I found myself *betwixt and between* those brothers on many occasions. And when in the company of the right people, I do not believe three's a crowd at all!" Constance gasped, her eyes bugged out, and she put her hands to her chest in shock.

"Celia Broadmore! I am amazed that you don't burst into flames just retelling that story," she sputtered. "You are so very, very awful! It's a wonder your Daddy didn't take after those boys with a shotgun and run them out of town himself. Lordy, girl! You are headed for eternal damnation. That is a given. But I guess you will go smiling and contented and skipping along the entire way!" Then we both broke out in laughter, as always, until we had tears in our eyes, eventually falling back in our seats exhausted from it all.

"I have to admit, I was just awful back then. I just wanted what I wanted and did not care about anyone else. I think I am a better person now." With my eyes looking up, I said, "Lord, I am trying to do better, trying all the time, and I hope that accounts for something when it is time to judge me. There are days that still provide me with a *substantial* struggle. Miss Constance, here, she helps me steer the boat a lot of times. Good friends speak the truth when we need it."

Constance smiled at me in understanding. She quickly added, "Celia, you need all the help you can get. I do not remember signing up for the job, but I most assuredly can tell you that I am glad to be here." Constance paused her talk, as if in thought, and then proceeded to change the subject. "You know, it was shortly after that night when my family moved to the Augusta area, and you and I first met."

"That's right! I met you about six months later at the holiday dance. That was the night Vernon first laid eyes on you. I think it was a done deal for you two before either of you had a clue what was happening, even though you did not marry until a several years later. Some days it does not seem that long ago at all."

"I know what you mean, Celia. I know what you mean. I still feel young inside, but the mirror reminds every day how old I really am, and it offers no forgiveness at all."

The train jerked forward, and once again we headed in the direction of Raleigh. In short time we would arrive, and I would finally see my family. My stomach was telling me that breakfast was wearing off. I suggested to Constance that we go for tea and cookies in the dining car. After checking our hair and appearance, off we went to enjoy our treats and the beautiful scenery of the North Carolina landscape.

Chapter 5

The cookies we were served were a mite stale. It did not matter though. Just being with my best friend was all that was necessary. We sat quietly for a few minutes, sipping tea and looking at the sights moving by our window.

I looked at my friend as she watched the scenery. Having one good friend as golden as her was such a gift. She was family as far as I was concerned. She was like a close sister I never had. The old gal was better preserved than me, by far. I know how hard she worked all her years, raising children and helping on the farm. Later she raised two of her grandkids until they turned eleven and twelve, when their daddy took them back. Constance rarely complained, always doing what had to be done, tending to everyone in the family, and not demanding anything in return. She had done all that and still looked fifteen years younger than me, but by birthdays she was seven years older. Must be in the genes, I thought, or something she ate as a child back there in Ohio. Walking by store windows these days, seeing my own reflection, I would always think, who is that *old* lady looking at me? I don't know her in the least. Then I would laugh and say to myself, "Better than being worm food, Celia." I would walk on with renewed gratitude in my heart that at my age I was still doing pretty good and still healthy. However, I secretly longed for the ageless beauty that Constance possessed.

With a lull in our talk and laugher, I realized Constance never got a chance to finish the story about the mysterious disappearance of her grandson's wife. She had started to speak of it just before Charlotte at the same moment Parker had appeared in all his glory. I felt bad that I had not remembered that until now, because she was clearly disturbed by the event when she first started to explain.

"Constance, dear, I did not get to hear the entire story about Emmett's wife. I'm sorry I did not remember until now. Please go on and tell me what this is all about. Is she still missing?"

She started with a heavy sigh. "Well, in the beginning we thought the girl had gone missin' and that there might have been evil at work. But as the details of her disappearance were slowly revealed, we found out otherwise. Poor Emmett," she said looking down at her hands. "Now he is questioning his manhood over all this. He has always had poor judgement when it comes to people, and marrying her was no exception. Vernon and I tried to change his mind about the marriage, but he is so strong willed. Takes after me, I guess, and his father too, for that matter. I always had a gut feeling that she was not right for him. Sadly, I was on point with that."

"What on earth do you mean? Why would he question his manhood?" I asked. "Did she leave him for another man? Is that it?"

"If it were that simple," Constance scoffed. "It is a mite more complicated than that, and something I am doing my best to try to understand, but I am still struggling with it all."

I asked the waiter for more tea as I could tell this was not going to be a short story. I patted Constance on the hand and asked her to continue. She began relaying the sequence of events leading up to the disappearance. She said she last saw Meredith about a week before Emmett was to return home from Dalton. The girl had stopped by to borrow some cinnamon spice. Constance felt this was just a pretense, because the young gal had seemed fidgety-like as she stood in the kitchen. As they talked, Meredith was up and down in her chair and even paced at times. Constance said she thought maybe she was pregnant and desperately wanted to tell someone, not wanting to wait until Emmett's return. Constance knew better than to ask. If this was the case, Emmett would be furious if others found out before he did. After some small talk, a glass of water, and a thank you, off she went to town. She claimed she had things she needed to purchase at Tipton's Variety before heading back home.

Constance said she just knew something just wasn't right. Her intuition was notoriously accurate. A few moments after the door banged shut, she said that she stepped to the window and looked down the road as Meredith walked away. She wondered what was going on with that girl. She was not acting normal. Constance was sure of that. While leaning her head gently on the window glass, she was surprised to see that Meredith had large bag by her side. It looked sort of like a travel bag. Constance just figured her eyesight was starting to fail, because why would Meredith be carrying luggage of sorts. Whatever kind of bag it was she must have left it outside on the porch and then picked it up upon leaving.

"That is the last I saw her," said Constance. "When Emmett came home, she was nowhere to be found. The house was completely empty and still when he walked in. Dishes were not washed. The bed was not made. The plant on the windowsill was almost dead from lack of water. Only a few of her clothes and personal items were missing, but not much really. It was so stressing to Emmett, the not knowing, for all of us really. It did not take long to find out though." Constance paused and looked down at the table again. I felt tense in my muscles as I waited for her to reveal the outcome of the missing wife. I moved in my seat a bit and leaned in to listen more.

"Celia, it would have been easier for Emmett to handle if she *had* left him for another man. Probably easier for me too, but I am not the one most affected by this mess, Emmett is. You see, the day after Emmett returned, we were all in a frenzy looking for her everywhere when a letter came in the mail for him. The return address was from a small town near New Orleans. I remembered her saying that she had family in that area. But now I think that was a lie of sorts."

Constance leaned in to whisper to me. "Celia, she left him alright, but it was for another *woman*. The letter told the story of her secret love from years past, and how she felt she could not be with Emmett anymore. She wrote that she needed to return to her love, or she felt she could never have happiness in her life." Constance stopped talking for a moment. I did not speak but waited for Constance to speak again.

"Lordy!" Constance said sharply and suddenly. "Doesn't a person know which way they want to ride in a saddle early on?" I could see her frustration and hurt on her face as she talked. "I mean, we are the way we are, and I am good with that. But why would she marry Emmett if that was not the life she wanted, or needed? It is the *why* she left that is causing Emmet to think it was his fault, that maybe he was not *man* enough somehow. Of course, we know that is bull crap! But he does not see it that way right now." She turned to look out the window.

"I do not rightly know why she would go ahead and marry him. She may have felt pressure to conform. Maybe she felt fear of what others might say or do, if it were known. The world will always include those deemed different by others, and by people who feel they have a right to judge and condemn them. You know how unkind and hateful some people can be when others do not fit their idea of what is right and proper. I, myself, have felt the condemning looks and heard the whispers of those self-appointed to judge, because they do not agree with how I have chosen to live my life. There are all sorts of reasons why Meredith may have felt the need to leave," I said. "I think she loved Emmett in her way, and she probably wanted him to have a better marriage and better life too."

"I bear her no ill will. It is just hard to see Emmett hurt," Constance admitted. It was tough for me to see Constance hurting. I laid my hand on hers to comfort her somehow. We sat in unusual silence again, each of us pondering the ramifications Meredith's actions.

The pause in our conversation made me remember someone that I had encountered numerous years ago. His name was Captain Eustace Marshall. It was a short affair, if you want to call it that. Captain Marshall was the kind of man who road *both* ways on his horse. After a short courtship, he suggested that we share a more physical closeness. Since I did not feel that kind of connection with him, I broke off our communication. I had no idea at the time that he also had *affection* for men, as well as women. I heard later through rumor that Captain Marshall regularly took *walks* with some of the men in his command, and that he was frequently caught *adjusting* many a man's uniform. Apparently, he was court-martialed for something similar to those allegations. When I heard this, I was not sure what to think. It perplexed me. I don't think I ever mentioned him to Constance. I let this thought fade quickly. My thoughts turned to the courage and depth of the love that Meredith must have had for her to leave a good man like Emmett. I looked over at Constance again. I tried to think of some words of wisdom or something I could say that might make her smile, and take the worry from her face.

"Emmett will hurt for a while, but some pretty gal will bring him back to the present someday, and he will forget all this happened," I said trying to sound positive and hopeful. "You will probably end up with a passel of great grandkids. Emmett the 2nd, Emmett the 3rd, Emmett the 4th, Emmetta Beth, a whole bunch of Emms pulling on your skirts," I said with a purposeful exaggeration in my voice. This got a little smile from Constance. It was always my nature to try to add humor to not so funny situations to break the tension. It was hard to see Constance quietly bear the weight of her family's troubles, but that was her nature. She loved hard and was very protective of all her children and grandchildren. I was glad my silly words had gotten her to break into a grin.

"I know you understand why she left. I know you have a forgiving heart. I also know how mean you can get when someone messes with your youngin's," I said. "Like the time when your boy, Benjamin, was being coaxed away from your side by that awful Mr. Smithfield. Remember how he particularly *liked* young boys and would try to lure them with hard candies and jellybeans? Everybody in town knew he was a pervert and a deviant. When in town, any mother with a young boy knew to keep a close watch on their young son. I will *never* forget the look on your face and what you said to him that day when you saw him giving Benjamin some candy."

Constance laughed and said, "I can laugh at it now, but I was not laughing in the least when that happened." I nodded in agreement.

"Oh, I know. You almost gave Benjamin whiplash when you jerked him back away from Mr. Smithfield. I knew instinctively to cover Benjamin's ears, because I could see the fire shooting out of your eyes. You got right in old Smithfield's face and told him if he came within a mile of your son again you would shoot off his nuts, make a necklace out of them, and hang it around his neck; nice and tight like." We snickered again.

"Indeed, I did! And I surely meant every word. I would die before I would let someone hurt my family, most especially a child. And from then on, I most certainly carried a pistol in my purse when I went to town. Thank goodness the Sheriff took care of that perverted, old bastard."

"Yes, amen to that, honey," I said as I raised a hand to the sky.

"Alrighty then, let's push those thoughts away now. How about we go gather our things and get ready for Raleigh. It shouldn't be too much longer before we get there."

"Sounds good," Constance replied. "I am already missing a real bed and some home cooking, and I am ready to be there. I have not seen your nephew in such a long time. I doubt I would recognize him if you weren't with me. Last time I saw him he was just sprouting whiskers."

As soon as Constance mentioned the word whiskers, for some reason I got a vision of Parker in his full beard; the way he looked when we first met. I always enjoyed it when a man wore his masculinity on the outside with a mustache or beard. I was shaken from this thought with a bark from Constance.

"Celia! Snap out of it! Let's get going!"

"Alright, old lady. I am coming right behind you. Just as well. There's no time for daydreaming right now. I was just being silly."

As we walked down the hallway of the train to our compartment, I could not help but feel excited to see my family. I desired to see Raleigh and the changes of the city since my last visit. There was a slight rush of adrenalin about the days ahead. I always looked at each day of my life as an adventure and as a gift. I had no idea about the adventures that Raleigh was about to deliver to me.

Chapter 6

Ten minutes later the long sounds of the train whistle indicated that we were pulling into Raleigh. "I can hardly wait to see them. I am excited and a bit nervous all at once. It has been so long. The last time I saw his daughters was when I came for Lila's wedding three years back."

We peered out our window to see if they were waiting for us, and they were. "There's my nephew, Amos, over there in the brown hat with those two gorgeous girls of his right next to him," I said, pointing in their direction. We smiled and began to wave. They spotted us in the window and waved back.

"Yes, yes, I see them," Constance said. "They are a good-looking bunch, Celia." Let's check our belongings and prepare to go. We are going to have a fine time here *for* sure."

As I stepped outside the train car door, my excitement increased. I stretched my arms in the air and began waving them about in the direction of my family and squealed with happiness. My exuberance caused me to lose my balance and down the steps of the train car I went, bumping my plump derriere on each step down, with a final landing on the platform of the train station. All this happened along with whoops and hollers from me and a scream from Constance. I heard people gasp and saw horrified looks on people standing nearby. My family quickly sliced through the crowd to come to my aid. I could hear Constance yelling from behind me.

"Celia, are you alright? Good lord almighty! You didn't break anything did you?"

"Well, this is quite a grand entrance isn't it," I said in a laugh. "Everybody in Raleigh now knows that I have arrived! They missed a good one if they weren't looking!"

Amos was already kneeling beside me and asked if I was hurt. The girls were fussing over me too. "Oh hell, I'm fine, nephew. Nothing hurt but my pride, thank goodness. All this and I haven't even been drinking yet today. Help me up please, Amos."

I stood with a bit of a wobble, and I brushed myself off while Constance checked my backside for dirt. She bushed at my skirt. I adjusted my hat which had flopped backwards in the ordeal. Lila picked up my purse and parcel and handed them to me. Grace was telling me to hold on to her if I felt unsteady.

"Good thing I have got lots of padding or that could have been problematic, to say the least."

"Celia, hold on the handrail next time and don't be so silly acting, please," sounding as if to scold me. "I am so glad you were not hurt, but you might be a tad sore tomorrow." My family nodded in agreement and uttered similar comments.

"It was a *minor* accident. I promise to be more careful, *mother*. Ok, now," I said, as I smoothed my clothes. "Let's start again. Come here and give your clumsy, Auntie Celia a big hug," as I reached out to grab all three of them at once. "I have missed you all so very much. It is such a joy to see each of you again. You girls have grown into the loveliest of young ladies. Don't you think so, Constance?" I said turning to look back at her. Then I took turns giving each one of them their own hug. How I wished they lived closer. I felt like I missed most their lives with them being so far away, with so few visits. Constance hugged each one too. She and I had known each other so long it was as if the family had her as an aunt as well.

Grace patted my arm and said, "Auntie Celia, thank you for coming such a long way to attend my graduation. This means so much me. The ceremony is not until ten on Friday morning, so we have several days to find some enjoyable and interesting things for you and Constance to see and do while you are here."

"That is wonderful, Grace. We are very happy to be here and spend time with you all. Please do not put yourselves out for us. We are easily entertained. Give Constance and I a place to sit and some Kentucky bourbon, and we will entertain ourselves for hours." Everyone laughed. The family was used to me being less than lady-like sometimes, and seemed to appreciate my sense of humor, *most* of the time. Just like Constance, they loved me warts and all.

"Auntie Celia, I will grab the luggage bags, and then we will head over to the house. My girls have fixed a lot of good food for us to enjoy," Amos said. "Grace made a cherry pie just for you."

"Thank you, Grace, dear. How sweet of you to remember that it is my favorite." I smiled at Grace and gently squeezed her hand.

"Works for my taste buds too," Constance offered.

We worked our way through the thinning crowd at the station and walked the four blocks to my nephew's beautiful, two-story home on Oak Street. Lovely magnolia trees adorned the front yard along with other flowering bushes and evergreens. It had such a welcoming presence as we strolled up the walkway. The lushness of the grounds felt very soothing and comforting to me. The perfume of jasmine welcomed us.

Amos had done well for himself and his family. He had gotten an education and was working as an architect. He was making a fine living. The girls had been given everything they needed to be successful in life themselves. Grace was graduating nursing school this week. She had no problem putting her love life on the back burner, as she pursued her passion for nursing. Her slightly older sister, Lila, was educated too. She had fallen in love with a captain in the Army, Samuel Akers, and had chosen to marry. She was of an artistic nature and loved to paint and sculpt. Lila and Samuel lived nearby in Holly Springs, so she saw her father and sister often. Lila would be staying at her father's house this week, while we visited, since Samuel was off to Washington on Army business again. He was not expected to return until after our departure. I hated that we would miss visiting with him on this trip. I had really hoped to get to know him better. Other than their wedding when I visited, I had not spent much time with him. He had a quiet nature, but I was determined to get to know his personality better. Lila seemed very happy with him and that is what mattered most.

The big white house had a grand porch with comfortable rockers, and I decided I must sit down and enjoy the porch view as soon as I arrived. Constance agreed. Neither of us wanted to admit that the walk had made us a little tired, since it had been mostly uphill. We chose the shady side of the porch in which to sit. We each picked a fan-back rocker and plopped down. Lila said she would go in and make some fresh sweet tea and bring it out to us. My nephew started to tote our luggage into the house, pausing in the doorway to say he would show us to our rooms later, after we rested a bit. Grace also went in to help Lila. I loved how those two girls often shared time together. You could always hear them frequently laughing together. The sound of their laughter always made me smile.

"This is a lovely town. I could easily live here. And this house is wonderful isn't it? We passed a lot of beautiful homes on our walk here." Constance definitely agreed and nodded her head so.

"I am lucky I could come and enjoy all this with you, Celia. Your family is so nice."

We both sighed in contentment as we rocked in the white wicker chairs. A light breeze arrived to cool us. After a few moments, I looked over at Constance and she had her eyes shut. She had already nodded off, and she was making a light puff sound each time she exhaled. She was much more delicate than me when she dozed. I tended to snort myself awake at times, or sleep with my mouth agape, and that surely was not something anyone wanted to see. I did my best not to nod off in front of other people, even my family.

The squeak of the screen door rousted Constance awake. The girls brought a silver tray that held small sweet cakes, tea, and a pretty pink rose from their garden. Constance and I clapped our hands and made sounds of delight, acting like little children. Lila said the small bites would hold us until our evening meal. Grace suggested that if Constance and I needed a nap before dinner that there was plenty of time for that. Amos appeared on the porch too, and he pulled up a chair next to us. We all joined in conversation about what was new in Raleigh since my last visit.

After almost an hour, and her eyelids getting a bit heavy, Constance stood and said, "I believe I will have me a little nap now. Please excuse me."

"Well, I think that sounds like a good idea. I'll go too. We older ladies need a tad more beauty sleep to keep us well preserved," I said, adding a smile and a wink.

Constance piped up. "I don't think the extra sleep is what is preserving you; I think it is all the bourbon you drink." The whole bunch of us laughed at her comment.

"Well now, I won't disagree. There is probably some truth in that. I guess you could call it my beauty secret!"

Amos started to rise in order to show us to our rooms. "Sit and rest, nephew, I remember my way around the house. Don't worry about being quiet down here either. When you get as old as us you sleep like babies again, anytime, anywhere, through all kinds of noise. See you in a little bit." In her comical way, Constance put her arm through mine, and off we went. That nap was sounding better by the minute. I would nap well if Parker stayed clear of my mind.

Dinner that evening felt so festive to me. I normally ate most meals alone. Having my best friend and family gathered around the table felt like a holiday meal. Lila and Grace had outdone themselves with all the food they prepared. I enjoyed the wonderful smells of fresh cooked sweet potatoes, green beans, and beets, all from their garden. Besides her studies, Grace was always in the garden puttering, pulling weeds, and planting things, and we were about to benefit from her efforts. Buttermilk biscuits hot from the oven were on the table, another of my favorite things. Amos had caught fresh fish earlier in the morning which we were all now enjoying in fine style. Fishing made him very happy and having his family enjoy his catch made it even better. Besides the special cherry pie, there were other sweets to tempt all of us. Lila's artistic talent showed in the artful decoration and display of the desserts, and in how beautifully she had prepared the table. It was hard not to want to eat everything in sight, but a gal's corset always convinced her otherwise. I always imagined my corset heaving a big sigh of relief when it was removed each time, due to trying to contain more than it should reasonably be asked to handle.

Our conversation stretched out dinnertime longer than normal. Eventually we all moved to the porch for an after-dinner sherry. The evening temperature was pleasantly perfect. Rays of late afternoon sunshine sprayed across the length of the porch, with just enough mild warmth to make a person feel good inside and out. Lila retrieved some candles in case we stayed out after dark.

"Auntie Celia, would you ladies like a day in the country while you are here?" Amos asked. "I know how you love being out in nature. We could take a picnic and go to the river for part of a day. I am sure you want to do some shopping as well. We can do as little or as much as you like while you are visiting.

62

I will take a day from work if you decide to go to the country so that I can join you. "

"I think both ideas sound very enjoyable. How 'bout you, Constance?"

"I agree...sounds good to me."

Before long the sun was gone, but we sat a while longer in conversation and watched the fireflies about the yard. Both cats had merged with us on the porch. The black and white one now rested in my lap, and the calico curled in contentment in Grace's lap. When Amos noted that both Constance and I had started to yawn, he announced that maybe it was time for everyone to retire for the evening. I rose from my chair with more soreness and stiffness than usual, a reminder of my bumbling departure from the train car. I kissed the girls and my nephew on the cheek and thanked the family for such a fine welcoming and wonderful meal. Constance did likewise. We said our goodnights and headed into the house and on up the stairs to our rooms.

Once in our room, I began my nightly ritual of writing in my journal. It was my way each day to get my thoughts and feelings out of my head in order to sleep easy. Constance took to her stitchwork in the same manner saying it calmed her mind before bed. I was relieved to just sit quietly together. After several minutes we yawned again, said goodnight to each other, and got into our beds. Sleep came quickly to Constance as I heard her puffing sound not long after she lay down.

My mind did not drop quickly into sleep. I listened to the evening crickets as I appraised the run-in with Parker this morning. All those years we were apart, and as soon as I saw him, I could not help but want him again. I had loved him. I still loved him. Just because someone has gone away does not mean you stop loving them. I felt I had been given a gift just to look into his eyes again. A tear now fell down my cheek. We do not always get second chances or even the glimpse of a second chance. I felt fortunate.

Although I never confessed it out loud, I secretly regretted pushing Parker out of my life. I felt too vulnerable and scared because of the intensity of my feelings for him, and how quickly they had come upon me. I did not trust myself or what I believed, because I was still recovering from the blow of deceit from that awful scoundrel, Clancy Jerdee. Clancy had taken advantage of me. He had fooled me into thinking he was a virtuous man when he was anything but virtuous. He had *used* my love. The depth of that wound made me question everything about myself for a while. I was still spinning from the betrayal when I met Parker. It was too soon for me trust myself, or anyone else. The timing could not have been worse for Parker. I heaved a long sigh. I was not going to let that jackass of man, Clancy, take up another second in my thoughts. Instead, I rolled over and quietly began to give the Lord my gratitude for the many blessings in my life. I also thanked him for the hope of a second chance with Parker.

Resting in the stillness, I flipped through some of the sugary memories with Parker. We were very much alike but enough different to make it both interesting and amusing. He was comfortable in his skin. He appeared to be at ease with my unconventional approach to life. He was definitely the *very finest* of all the chocolates. I took a slow, deep breath and released it with a slow ease. I closed my eyes and sighed. The crickets continued to serenade me until I was dreaming and in deep slumber, along with Constance.

Chapter 7

I moved a little slower as I eased out of bed the next morning. My tailbone was a mite tender from my less than acrobatic dismount from the train. Less sitting and more moving would probably work it out and make it feel better, I thought. Constance noticed my slow movements. I suggested that maybe walking to town for shopping and some lunch would be the best thing to do this day. She easily agreed.

It was mid-morning before we completed our beautifications and headed downstairs to the kitchen for coffee and a light breakfast. Amos had already left for work hours before. He diligently arrived earlier than necessary at his workplace. He was always extra dedicated which was one reason he was so successful. Grace had left too, because she had early practice for the ceremony on Friday. Lila was busy in the kitchen already working on preparations for tonight's dinner.

"Good morning, Auntie, Constance. Sleep well?" Lila asked.

"Yes, good morning, Lila. We slept just fine and dandy. Didn't we, Constance?"

"We sure did. I think I was asleep before my eyes went shut." And the day began with laughter.

"I will take your coffee to the dining room and then fix you some breakfast", Lila said.

"Oh sweetie, don't bother with all that this morning. We'll just sit here in the kitchen with our coffee and visit with you. And I think for breakfast all we would like is one of those leftover biscuits of yours and some strawberry jam. How does that sound, Constance?"

"Just perfect, Celia. That is especially so if we plan to take lunch in town today."

"You ladies are definitely easy to please," Lila said, as she moved about the kitchen to bring us coffee and our requested breakfast. She proceeded to tell us about the best shops downtown and where we might find a satisfying lunch. We thanked her for serving us and making us feel so welcome. We proceeded to gather our purses and parasols for our trip to town.

"Feeling good enough to make the walk, Celia?" Constance asked.

"Oh definitely. I think I will loosen up just fine if I keep moving today." Off we went in a casual stroll. The sun was bright and hot. No clouds in the sky. We used our parasols immediately for shade. If rain came, we would be set for that too.

Within three blocks of walking east, we approached the business area of town. We could hear fiddle music. A sidewalk musician was playing a light-hearted tune on the corner by the bank. Constance and I both dropped some coins in his fiddle case, thanked him for the lovely sounds, then continued on to find the milliner's shop. Constance was in need of a new hat and this would be the perfect city to find one. East coast styles made their way to Raleigh even sooner than Augusta.

We found the shop just two doors down from the bank. The bell on the door handle tinkled with sound as we opened it and when inside. We were greeted by a pleasant-faced owner who invited us to browse the hats she had on display. She noted that if we were not in a big hurry that she could also custom make a hat, if that was our choice. We thanked her, but said our time in Raleigh was limited, and that would not be an option for us on this trip. Constance spotted a deep blue satin one with feathers that she was immediately enamored with it. She almost sprinted towards it as if it might jump up and leave if she did not grab it quickly. Trying it on, she grinned, and said that she loved it. I agreed she looked beautiful in it. The color made the blue in her eyes even more intense. I was sure Vernon would notice that. She placed it back on the stand and engaged in looking around a bit more. She needed to be sure that it was right one, and not rush to a decision. The brown one was too dull. The green one, though stunning, was too pricey. When she tried the blue one on the second time, it no doubt made her very happy. The blue satin hat was going home with her.

I delighted in seeing Constance smiling and happy, and excited about her purchase. I looked around at all the hats too, but I found nothing that I felt I needed to buy. The owner carefully wrapped tissue around the hat then placed it in a very attractive hat box. Constance commented how she had not spent money on herself in a while. She said Vernon had told her to get something nice for herself when in Raleigh, and this was going to be her special purchase. She had accomplished it in lickety-split time. We continued our exploration of Raleigh with Constance clutching the braid handle of the hat box with both her hands.

As we leisurely ambled down Main Street, we came upon a small business just off on a side alley. The sign said, "Fortune Telling, Palm Reading, and Tarot Cards." It had a small black door that looked slightly ominous.

"Constance, look there," I said pointing to the sign. "Let's go in and have our fortunes told. It will be fun!"

"Oh lordy, Celia. They will just trick you out of your money, girl. They probably talk in generalities and such so what they say could apply to anyone who comes in the door."

"Oh, I know it is make-believe, but it will be fun just to see what they say. Awww, come on. Pretty please."

"Ok, ok. I'll go, but just for you. I do not care to have my palm read or a phony fortune told." And with hearing that, I grabbed Constance by the hand and pulled her reluctantly in the direction of the door. With a gentle push on the unlatched door, we quietly stepped into a darkish room.

Entering the business from the bright outdoors made it difficult to see at first. The curtains were mostly closed, so only small of amounts of daylight were welcomed in the very small room. We stood just inside the door while our eyes adjusted.

Constance nudged me and said, "You sure you want to do this, Celia?"

"Yes, I do," trying to sound confident, but feeling not so sure. "Let's see what this is all about."

A small, shrunken woman appeared out of a back room and slowly shuffled towards us. Her stringy gray hair swayed as she walked. Her skin was almost grayish in color and very thin looking. If it had been nighttime, I might have thought her a ghost, as she took on the appearance of such. She spoke to us without raising her head to look at us. She directed us to sit at the table.

"What is it you want today?" she asked in a slow, scratchy voice. "Do you want your fortune told, have your palm read, or do you want me to read your tarot cards?"

"Well, I believe I would like you to tell my fortune, if you would please," I answered.

"That will be ten cents. I always like to take care of the business part first. Sometimes people are shaken after hearing their fortunes, and they have run out on me before paying."

"Sounds like a smart plan." I replied. "I am happy to oblige." I laid out the coins which she quickly grabbed and pushed into her pocket.

"Relax in your chair. This may take a few minutes. Place your hands, palms down, in the middle of the table. Sit quietly. No talking."

Constance nudged her elbow against my arm as if to say without words, "Are you believing this hooey?" I ignored the nudge and focused on the age lines of the woman's face, doing my best not to say anything, which had always problematic for me. The old woman seemed to be taking this all very seriously, so I dare not act a fool while she worked.

She placed her thin-skinned hands on top of mine, closed her eyes, and lowered her head. Her chin was almost on her chest. She held this pose for what seemed like several minutes. I looked at Constance and silently mouthed the word, sleeping, with a questioning look on my face. I was trying to convey the question of whether the old lady had fallen asleep or not, without breaking the no talking rule. Constance shrugged and shook her head as if to say she was not sure. I was starting to feel a little uneasy. Being that she was so old, I feared she might have just died while sitting there. Suddenly the woman's head snapped up with her eyes still closed, and she began to speak. The scratchiness of her voice made me wince.

"I keep seeing the shape of a heart; a heart that is being kept in darkness or perhaps a box. There is something around the heart...a rope...a chain. I am not sure. But the heart is being contained somehow. It is not living as it should." I looked at Constance and she still showed signs of disbelief on her face. Her mouth was twisted up and her eyebrows in a frown. I turned back to watch the woman's face. I did not really understand what she was trying to relay to me. The woman continued speaking, and her eyes remained closed.

"I am also seeing a uniform of some kind...wait....it is a soldier in a uniform." Constance kicked me slightly under the table, but I fought the temptation to acknowledge it, staying focused on the old woman. "The soldier is reaching for something." I felt another little kick from Constance which I still ignored. This was starting to hit close to home. I assumed the old lady meant Parker, and I knew that is probably what Constance's kick meant. I was a little nervous about what she might say next.

"There is a strong connection between the soldier and you. It has been broken, though, broken for many years. There is also a strong energy, an unknown force, that wants you and the soldier to come together in the same place. The force, whatever it is, is good in nature." I looked at Constance with my eyes wide open. I was shocked at what the woman had just said. Constance looked at me in the same manner. I knew we both wanted desperately to squeal, but we could not. Our faces expressed what we could not say out loud.

I turned my eyes back to the woman. She dropped her head to her chest once more. Her eyes remained closed. Again, we waited for what seemed like minutes. She heaved a big breath and then a second one. Then she raised her head again with her eyes still closed.

"I see the letters, P and B, above the soldier, and they are moving around him," she said softer, almost as a whisper. I heard a slight noise from Constance just then, but I did not dare look at her. I was fixated on the old lady's face now, not believing how she could know these things, and desiring to hear more. How could she possibly know about Parker?

Then the old woman began to hum to herself, then paused, then she spoke. "The soldier and the heart should be brought together. This I am told should happen, by the force, the energy, the goodness," she said. She breathed again and opened her eyes. She stared straight at me for several seconds, then finally blinked and said, "I hope you understand." Then she simply got up and hobbled into the back room again. Nothing more was said.

I spun sideways in my chair to face Constance. We grabbed and squeezed each other's hands. Our eyes open wide in amazement. We were both still trying to contain our reactions and not make any noise.

I motioned to Constance to get up and go and gently pushed her towards the door. As soon as the door shut, she squealed, and I squealed. "What on earth!" I exclaimed. "How could that bruja-witch have known about Parker, about the two of us being separated?" I gasped.

"Celia, I was a disbeliever when I walked in and I came out with chills up my spine. The hair on my arms is standing straight. That old woman has a gift, I do believe. And here Parker showed up out of the blue on the train!" she said at almost a shout. "The Lord is working his magic! He's telling you something, Celia. You had better listen this time."

"Goodness gracious, Constance. I am definitely flustered by what she said but that does not mean a thing, really. I cannot talk right now. Hell, I can barely catch my breath." We paused our talking and each of us took a deep breath, then we looked at each other, and squealed out loud again. "This just makes my stomach knot up, Constance. Am I really supposed to get back with Parker? I just cannot believe what is happening on this trip! What force is she talking about?"

"Celia, do you have to be knocked over the head? Everything in the world is lining up for you to have a second chance with Parker. The energy or the force she talked about is the Almighty, for Pete's sake. I am a bit surprised he is being so good to you with all your *zestfulness* and such, all these years. I guess he knows you are good at heart, even though you sometimes try to hide that part of yourself. You deserve to be happy, Celia. Sometimes I think you don't believe that. I think you push love away when you should be thankful it showed up at all. I think it is minor a miracle. I think the Lord wants you to get married, Celia."

"Oh goodness me," I sighed. "Ok," I said, grabbing Constance by her shoulders. "Here's what's going to happen. Do not, and I repeat, do not utter a word of this to my family. You promise?" Constance frowned but nodded her head in agreement. "I do not need others besides you telling me I ought to run off and get married. Really? At my age? Marriage? We just won't talk of it anymore. And that is that. This will be our secret. Agreed?"

Constance scowled at me but nodded agreement. "You know that is going to be a downright difficult and painful promise for me to keep, but I will do my best. I am liable to burst a blood vessel or something else in me. I promise I will not say a word. Not a peep, even if it pains me."

I pulled out my fan and began waving it back and forth while trying to regain my composure. I suggested we start walking again and just not talk for a few minutes. I just needed some quiet right now. We headed from the alley to the main walkway again. We turned the corner to our right and immediately came to a quick stop as we almost ran into two policemen who did not see us coming either. All of us paused in surprise. We all took a step backwards, because we were almost touching toes when we came to a stop. Luckily, we had avoided physically bumping into each other.

"Please excuse us ladies," said the man with the mustache. "We were deep in conversation and did not hear you approaching."

The other man nodded and said, "Yes, please excuse us. Our apologies for not paying more attention to others on the street."

"Oh, no problem, officers. We were deep in thought ourselves. I am glad we all did not collide and bump heads," I said. I followed up the statement with my best lady smile.

"I don't believe that I have seen you ladies in town before. Are you visiting someone?" said the mustache man.

"Well yes, we are visiting my nephew and his family. We are from Augusta, Georgia. Your town is quite lovely."

"Well thank you, ma'am. Please allow me to introduce ourselves. I am the chief of the police department here in Raleigh, and my name is Percy Bordeaux. This is my first captain, Paxton Backfish."

"Pleasure to meet you," said Paxton, nodding at us again.

Constance let out a tiny squeak when he said their names, and her eyebrows went up, and they stayed up. I knew exactly what she was thinking. I tried my best not to look shocked and to stay composed. The fortune teller talked about a uniform and the letters P and B. She did say soldier though. These men were not soldiers, at least not in the military sense. Good lord, were we in another dimension? I thought. Here were men in uniform and both had the initials, P.B. What in the world was going on? I surely thought this could not possibly be happening to us. We were sure the old lady was talking about Parker Boyd. My head began to spin. I just could not believe the events of the moment. I was glad Constance was here for verification.

"Ma'am, are you ok? You look a mite rosy in the face," said Chief Bordeaux.

"Ah, yes, we're both fine. Just a little warm. Um...we are heading for some tea and some lunch," I managed to say without spitting. "Oh, where are my manners? My name is Celia Broadmore and this is my wonderful, best friend, Constance Willoughby."

"Yes, indeed it is a pleasure to meet you ladies. Is your nephew Amos Broadmore, ma'am?" Chief Bordeaux asked. He paused for an answer with a slight smile on his face.

"Yes, he most certainly is. I am so very proud of him."

"I know Amos from our work on the city planning committee. I may just have to stop by while you ladies are visiting, so that we may continue our conversation. Please let me know if there is anything that I can assist you with while you enjoy your stay in Raleigh. Have a lovely afternoon. I hope we will see each other again before you depart." And with that both officers nodded, moved around us, and went on their way.

Constance and I stood still for a few moments. Constance squeezed my forearm in almost a pinching fashion after the officers passed. We did not look at each other. I took her elbow and pushed her forward, and we continued in silence. We crossed the street at the corner. Then we stopped and turned to look at each other.

Constance immediately blurted out, "Good lord, Celia! You have got PB's running all around you. I cannot believe this just happened. Maybe it wasn't Parker the old gal was talking about. Maybe you were meant to find someone new right here in Raleigh. Maybe it was not a soldier's uniform but a policeman's uniform. She could have made a mistake on the interpretation. If this don't beat all...goodness me! Kind of unnerving isn't it?"

"Constance, don't go getting silly, crazy about this. It is very strange, but I cannot start acting like a schoolgirl just because of coincidence." I was trying to get a grip on the situation. I pulled my fan out again and started waving it at a fevered pace.

"It does beat all, though. Let's go have lunch. I think we will calm down a bit once we get something in our stomachs. Do you have any whiskey in your purse?" I asked. "Lord, I could use a nip right now. It would help to calm my nerves a tad. That commander was a handsome sort though, wasn't he? I would guess that he is close to my age. Oh heavens, let's go eat and take a break from all this silliness. I am really starting to regret the fortune teller idea now. There's a whole lot of craziness in the air."

Up the street we went. We could see the restaurant's red and white sign just a short distance away. We went inside and were seated nicely by the window where we could watch passersby. It felt good to sit and be calm for a minute. The young waiter walked up to the table announced that his name was Patrick, and he said he would be taking care of us today. I looked at Constance and she looked at me, and we smiled at each other. We both knew exactly what the other one was thinking. I had to ask. "Patrick, if you don't mind, may I ask what your last name is?".

"Oh no problem, ma'am. My last name is Belcamp."

Constance muted a chuckle into her napkin, but my laugh escaped quite loudly. The waiter naturally looked perplexed at our outburst of laughter. I assured him it was nothing funny about him or his name, but just a funny coincidence we were experiencing this day with names. "Ignore our silliness, Patrick. We are just two silly old ladies."

We ordered a lunch of cucumber sandwiches, tea, and fresh tomato slices with a sweet glaze. "I sure hope today has no more surprises in store. I prefer dull, boring, and normal, please."

Constance was focused on her plate as we continued to talk. "Well, I don't know about that, Celia. That policeman may show up at your nephew's house." Constance seemed amused at the possibility. I could see her delight in the wrinkling up of her crow's feet around her eyes, as she tried to stifle a smile. "I surely would not want to miss that moment." She paused her eating to look up and me, as she dabbed her smiling mouth with her napkin.

"Mercy me, Constance. I think he was only making polite small talk. It has nothing to do with that old fortune teller. How I am already regretting that idea. Can we let this go now, please? Let's do a bit more shopping, and then we can head back to the house," I said.

"Sounds fine to me," Constance replied. We paid our bill, thanked our waiter for obliging us, and left the restaurant.

We proceeded to walk towards the direction of my nephew's house, window shopping on the way. I purchased some candies in the general store to share with the family. Constance bought some honey. We decided a little nap sounded good, so we strolled on back to the house.

No one was home when we arrived. Instead of going upstairs, the nice breeze and the rockers on the porch suited us just fine for napping purposes. Both cats appeared and hopped up on the porch to join us. Each one found a sunspot to laze on. All four of us dozed in blissful, easy sleep within minutes.

Chapter 8

When a fly started buzzing my ear, I awoke in annoyance. I saw that my nephew was just pulling up in a flatbed wagon in front of the house. The sound of the wagon and horses jarred Constance and the cats awake. I waved at Amos.

"What's with the wagon, Amos," I said.

"I got it down at the livery stable. I thought we would need it for all of us to go to the river tomorrow for our picnic. It should hold all of us and everything we need to take."

"You hear that Constance? Tomorrow we get a day in the country and a picnic by the river." Constance let out a two-fingered whistle, and we both clapped our hands like little kids.

Amos chuckled at our response, and he shook his head in amusement. "I thought that would make you two happy. Did you ladies have an enjoyable time in town today?" Constance elbowed me and I ignored her. I was glad Amos had not seen her do that. I frowned at her, and I held my finger to my lips reminding her to be quiet about today's strange events.

"Yes indeed," I answered loudly. "Constance even found herself the perfect hat, and she looks beautiful in it. We also did some other shopping and had a pleasurable lunch too. We both purchased some sweets at the general store for you and the girls. Nothing exciting happened at all, just a nice stroll about town."

Amos nodded in reply, as he fussed with the horses. "I suspect those girls have supper just about done by now. You ladies head on in and see what's cookin'. I am going to put the wagon and horses in the barn, and then I will be in myself."

"Alrighty then," I replied. Lord knows I shouldn't miss a meal. I wouldn't want to go getting too thin and scrawny now," I said while patting my more than ample hips. The screen door banged shut after we went inside, leaving the two cats sitting and staring, looking as if they were expecting an invitation to go inside too.

Dinner that evening was a delight to the senses, the ears, and the heart. Amos filled us in on his new project for the university. He would be on a team of architects to build a new library. This announcement got a round of applause from the whole group. Grace talked of her graduation on Friday. She seemed thrilled to start her career as a nurse. She had already inquired into possible work upon graduation. I knew her caring nature and diligence would make her good at her profession. Lila spoke of her desire to create a local museum of natural history, which was something I had no idea she had even thought about. As I sat and listened to their accomplishments and desires, I could not have felt more pride than if they had all been my children. Amos had worked so hard in his education and career. He had made sure his girls were educated too, and now the girls were blossoming. His good guidance, plus their education, had started the girls off in life as best as anyone could hope.

I spoke up after they finished talking. "I am so very happy that you three have been able to extend your education past the basics. You make me so proud, and I most certainly brag on each of you every chance I get. You know, I too, have always felt blessed to have been given a college education. My daddy made sure of that. I wish higher learning could be available to anyone who desires it." All at the table nodded in agreement.

Constance snickered to herself and said, "Celia, did you ever tell them how your daddy was able to send you to college, even though at that time he was experiencing trouble with some of his investments, and was not sure how he would pay for it all?"

"No, I don't believe I ever have. Not quite sure that it would be appropriate dinner conversation, but since you brought it up, and we are all family and friends, I guess I could tell the story. It is not a very *genteel* subject, but a true story though," I said laughingly.

"Auntie Celia, I do not think subject matter has ever stopped you from talking before. I do not think *anything* has ever stopped you from talking," Amos teased. Constance let out a hoot, and everyone laughed.

"He has got you there, Celia. He has a big dose of your wit."

"Oh, you are as ornery as I am sometimes, Amos! Well anyway, as you know, my daddy was a smart man. He knew very well not to put all his eggs in one basket. He had multiple business dealings during his life, some went well, some not so good, and some downright failed. A year before I went to college, my father's investments were down, way down, and money was more than tight. He fretted how he would send me to college. He too, felt education was a top priority, and that it should be available to all. That is when he decided to take what savings he had and buy the best damn bull he could find in the country, which he did. He had it shipped from the east coast. He really had no intention of raising a lot of cattle, only a few just for our purposes."

Lila spoke up and inquired, "Why would he want to spend so much money on a bull if raising cattle was not his intent?"

"Well, my sweet Lila, there are other money-making options when you own a champion bull, my dear. Daddy knew where the money was at, and it was not necessarily in raising cattle. His idea was to sell the *bull squirt* and use the money for my college." Everyone at the table snickered at this, even me. "That was some expensive *bull squirt* coming from the second-best champion bull in the country!" I said smiling. "People came from all around for it. Yes, indeed. It paid for my college tuition, my living accommodations, as well as clothes and food, and probably more on top of that."

I leaned forward a bit, as if I was about to tell a secret. All eyes were on me. I raised my eyebrows a tad and said, "You know, I never dared ask my father about any of the *particulars* on the *collection* of the commodity, so to speak. But I did wonder about the logistics when the *squirt* was *harvested* and sold without the arrival of a cow on the farm for natural insemination. I realized long ago, some things in life do not need to be discussed. My *imagination* filled in the details, I guess you could say. However, I did say to father one time, that whoever he hired to *collect* the bull squirt should definitely be paid highly for this unsavory, and *very* dangerous job." Laughter spilled into the room again.

"Celia, you are so full of it sometimes! You always manage to add such extra *embellishments* to your stories! It is a good thing that we all love you and do not mind your colorful sense of humor," Constance said with her usual smart-ass grin attached to the comment.

Amos pushed back his chair once he stopped laughing. "Tomorrow we will head out for the river around 9 a.m. Is that alright with you ladies?" We all nodded in agreement and said yes.

"In that case, I think Constance and I will head on upstairs to journal and do some stitchwork before retiring."

"Alright then. Good night Auntie, Miss Constance," Amos said as he nodded in our direction. "I think we are all looking forward to going to the river tomorrow. You know how I *love* to fish. Sleep well, and we shall see you in the morning," he said. He left and headed towards the library room. The girls bid us goodnight too. They said would be up shortly. They still needed to finished the dishes and feed the cats.

The house was soon quiet with only the whippoorwills and crickets making noise. I often regretted that I could not stay awake as long as I wanted to listen to these sounds; they were so calming to me. We did not journal or stitch. We were too tired from this bizarre day. As we turned out the lights, and got into our beds, we heard the annoying screech of a cat fight break into the tranquility of the night.

"Thanks for keeping quiet about the fortune teller and all the PBs we ran into today."

"Lips are sealed. You know I keep my word."

"Sleep well, old lady," I said to Constance.

"You too, you old bag of bones."

We both giggled like little girls. Each of us let out a big sigh. I had one brief, sweet thought about Parker and when I might see him again before we both quickly nodded off in sleep, with no effort required.

Chapter 9

Like a child on Christmas, I awoke early. I did my best not to disturb Constance, but I found that she was awake before me. We were both exhilarated about the trip today. Constance was the first child in her family, and her daddy treated her more like a son than a daughter. She was taught early on how to fish, hunt, and take care of herself in the woods. She did everything with her daddy that a son would do. Constance learned to love the outdoors because of this. She most assuredly loved to fish, so today was going to be her kind of day.

I personally never cared if I caught a fish or not. For me, it was more about soaking up fresh air and sunshine, and the feeling of being rejuvenated and bathed by nature. Nature was my church, and my way of finding balance. Of course, if my supper depended upon catching a fish, then I most certainly did care about catching one. Instead of holding a fishing pole, it was more likely you would find me lying on my back looking up at the clouds, searching for colorful rocks or plants, or digging for arrowheads. I always carried a sack with me when venturing into the woods. I never knew what treasures I would discover in nature and would want to bring home. I had snatched up an old flour sack off of the pantry shelf to bring with me today.

Upon arrival at the river, I would *definitely* have my shoes off, skirts hiked, and be wading in the water straight away.

The smell of cooked bacon brought my nose and my mind back to the morning. The allure of this scent caused both us to get ready with haste. We were downstairs in record time. Lila and Grace once again made sure we ate well, and we did our best to oblige them. With coffee, bacon, and potato cakes in our bellies, out the door we went.

Amos had thoughtfully placed a wooden box near the wagon to assist us old ladies in climbing into the back. Straw bales had been added for seats. Constance and I did not mind that a bit. We were country girls at heart. Lila brought the basket of lunch goodies, and Grace retrieved blankets for us to sit on for our picnic, and for lounging about. I had my treasure sack on my lap, along with my sun hat. I figured I would find me a walking stick from on old tree branch once we got to the river, and then my outdoor ensemble would be complete. Amos called out, "All aboard, this wagon train's leaving the station now!" We all hollered and cheered! We were all ready for a day in the country.

A short distance outside of town, in flat stretch in the road, we spied an unusual wagon with a wooden top. It was progressing in our direction. It turned out to be one of those *gypsy* wagons. As a child they always scared me, because my daddy had always warned me to stay clear of any gypsies. He never really explained why. As it passed, we waved and said hello to the dusty looking man at the reins. He waved with little animation, and he did not speak at all. After it moved by us, I noticed a tiny, old lady looking out the back window. She spoke as I looked at her. "Do what you know you must," she said in her aged voice. I leaned backwards in surprise at this.

Constance grabbed my arm. "Did she say you are turning to dust?" The girls giggled loudly at the question.

"No," I chuckled, "but that is not far from the truth at my age. I think she said, do what you know you must. Sounds strange to me," I said, shaking my head at the statement. "What the heck is that supposed to mean?" I asked. Grace spoke and confirmed that old woman indeed said what I thought I had heard. I suggested the woman might not be mentally all together. Constance had a different take on what the old woman had said.

"Celia, maybe she is psychic, you know," as she nudged my elbow. "Maybe she sensed something about you. Some of those gypsies have clairvoyant gifts, or so I have heard tell."

I knew what Constance meant. We had known each other so long; it was almost like we were on the same brain wave. I knew she was implying that the woman was somehow giving me the same message as the fortune teller in town. "Oh hush, girl, that is just silly," I scoffed. "You have a wild imagination sometimes, Constance."

"I think you mean intuition. I have intuition, Celia. You know I do," she said with a good bit of sass in her voice. "You have said that about me a hundred times over. Have I ever been wrong?" I frowned a tad. I had to admit she was right. She did have a gift in that way.

"It doesn't matter anyway. That old lady is on her way to somewhere else, and I won't have a chance to confirm your *intuition* theory."

"Things work in mysterious ways sometimes, Celia. Mys-teri-ous ways," Constance repeated, slowly drawing out the words. Then she smiled and winked at me. Grace and Lila giggled at our repartee of our friendly words, and how we teased at each other as we bounced about in the wagon.

Luckily, I was able to distract them from the topic by pointing out flowers of this and that kind. I got them to try to identify the sound of particular birds. Halfway to the river, Amos signaled to us that there was a Cooper's hawk nearby. Later on the trail, we spied two deer grazing at the back of a sunny open area. After they gave a quick glance our way, the deer seemed to pay us no mind. Even though we were riding in a less than luxurious wagon, the ride was remarkably pleasant. How could it not be? There was sunshine, the smells of nature, critters and birds, and the joy of spending the whole day with my family and best friend. As I had this thought, the wagon jerked to a stop. We were at our destination before I realized how far we had traveled.

"Yeehaw! Time to fish!" Amos shouted, as he hopped down from the seat. In gentlemanly fashion, he came around and helped each of us ladies off the wagon. "Can you ladies handle the rest of the things?" he asked. We all answered with an affirmative. With a big grin on his face, Amos immediately turned and grabbed his fishing pole and creel, and then he headed off down to the river, mumbling something about seeing us for lunch in a while. I observed a Catalpa tree nearby. I knew he would make stop there to pluck some worms from it to use for bait. Good bait for bluegills, or so I had been told.

As I stood and surveyed the area, I could clearly see this spot by the river was no doubt designed by God. It was glorious! Simply glorious! The kind of place you did not want to leave, with big ol' shade trees of various varieties, lush grasses, the crystal-clear river, and wildflowers growing in abundance. There were areas to the east and west, as if planned, where one could see both the sunrise and sunset. So many hues of Nature's green for the eye to see. I watched the cat's-paw ripples on the slow-moving river and the fluffs from cottonwoods that floated about as I viewed the landscape. If I had any artistic talent, this is how I would paint my heaven. I thought as though I could breathe this beauty into my lungs. Hoping to keep the memory forever inside me, I closed my eyes and breathed deeply what I had just witnessed. Maybe Lila could capture it with paint and brush, so that I could hold it in my hands to recall this day; this spectacular moment of life.

The weather we had been given for the day was close to perfect. With the sun rising higher, it got a bit drippy warm, though. However, wading in the river would cool us right down. We ladies busied ourselves putting down the blankets and baskets. As soon as all that was taken care of, off came my shoes and socks, and I grabbed my flour sack. I headed to the river to wade about and to look for rocks and fossils.

"Last one to the river is a dirty duck!" I yelled, as I pretended I was going to run. I had already learned that there is a point in life where running is not really an option for those with significant age. Running for the more mature should be saved for an emergency, or for pure survival from harm or threat, so if you did see me running, then you'd better run too! I simply hobbled at a good rate to avoid eating dirt or twisting an ankle. Constance was lucky that she was still nimble. She was almost running. She was right behind me chiding me that she could get there faster than I could. We were followed closely by Grace and Lila who seemed to enjoy our old-lady shenanigans. We were cackling and laughing, as we waded out into the water. This was a perfect spot, shallow but with a profusion of smaller rocks that did not hurt our feet. In no time we were all bent over and culling the water for treasures. I imagined we all looked like some strange cluster of birds. We were bent over, with our heads pointing down, and our hind ends in the air, standing in a line. I had to snicker at the image in my mind.

We all heard it at the same time. The wagon horses made some noise as though they had been disturbed. In unison, as if doing a planned, synchronized movement, we all rose up and twisted to our left to look behind us to see the cause of the problem. There was a gentleman on horseback near the wagon. He waved and shouted a friendly hello. I squinted as if that would help me see him better. My mouth dropped open when I realized it was that policeman, Percy Bordeaux, that Constance and I had run into downtown.

"Celia, that's the policeman we met the other day! Oh boy, this is going to get interesting," Constance said amusingly. She twisted her mouth into a slight contortion at what might be about to happen.

"Hush it now, Constance. Do not let your imagination go crazy."

Grace and Lila looked perplexed, as they realized they did not know the whole story, whatever it might be. They listened to us chatter back and forth. Chief Bordeaux got down from his horse and tied it up. We ladies quickly exited the river and dropped our skirts so as to remain proper in front of the visitor.

"Hello, ladies," he said, as he removed his hat and approached.

"Chief Bordeaux, what a wonder it is to see you way out here," I said. He nodded in gentlemanly fashion.

"Yes," he said, "it is unusual that we meet up again out here. I ride out here at least once a week. It clears my mind to be out here and get away from the city. I just did not expect to run up on anyone. Did Amos come with you as well?"

"Oh, yes. He ran off as fast as he could to fish and get some peace and quiet. I am sure he needed to get some distance from all the lady jabber," I replied. I felt Constance's presence right behind me. "You remember my friend, Constance?" I said as I turned towards her and made a face at her as if I were distressed. I did it at such an angle so that neither the chief nor the girls could see my face.

He nodded and smiled. "Miss Constance, hello again," and then looked past her to speak to the girls. "Hello, Miss Grace, Miss Lila, how have you young ladies been lately?"

They shared some small talk then Lila asked if Chief Bordeaux would like to join us for the picnic. She announced that she was positive she packed more than enough food, and we would be happy to share. I swallowed hard at hearing this. I prayed he would say no. I did not want Constance nudging me the entire time he was here. And frankly, I had no interest in him as Constance might have thought, even though he was a fine cut of a man. I was still frequently thinking of seeing Parker and what might come of that, but I was not telling anyone, not even Constance. Graciously he declined the offer. He said he had to transport a prisoner to the train a little later and had to head on back to town. Covering it with a smile, I sighed in relief.

"It was a very pleasant surprise to see you here, Miss Celia, and you, Miss Constance, and your lovely nieces. It is my hope that we might meet up again before your departure, perhaps for dinner, as my guests. I must get back to work now. Enjoy the rest of your day. Too bad I cannot stay and maybe do some *fishing* myself," he said with a wink and smile in my direction. Then with a tip of his hat, he swung into the saddle, turned his horse towards town and trotted off.

The girls and Constance were giggling before he got out of ear shot. I turned quickly to shush them, but the request was ignored. I relinquished to laughing along with them. Then I picked up a stick, raised it in the air as if to chase them, and they ran all the way back into the river amid the laughter.

Absent of any grace, I stumbled and fell into the water, but I was not injured. I embraced the moment, and I turned and plopped my backside in the water and just sat there. I laughed loudly, as did the others. "Well look here, it is so much easier to find the best ones if you are closer to the water!" as I grabbed a stone with pink and silver sparkles, and displayed it in my hand. Our laughs filled the air and I am sure Amos could hear all our hee-hawing and splashing. I thought Chief Bordeaux might change his mind about dinner if he could see me now, sitting in the water, my hair a mess, and laughing as loudly as a mule. And then I thought to myself, not Parker, he would be sitting in the water with me. I smiled inside and felt my heart strings pulled by memories of him. I briefly thought of those moonlit nights of skinny dippin' and summer lovin'. I wished I could transport myself back to that time once more, even if only for a few ephemeral moments.

Constance and the girls were singing now and it brought me back to the present. I joined in while I stood to wring my petticoats and find a large boulder to sit on. I spread my skirts about the rock hoping they could dry some before lunch. Constance decided to go fishing. She now occupied herself with finding some worms and getting her pole ready. The girls continued their wading and rock searching until Amos appeared about an hour later.

"I'm pretty hungry, ladies. Shall we eat?" Amos said as he rubbed is belly.

"I know my stomach's ready," Constance replied without missing a beat. For such a small gal she sure could eat a lot of food, and she always seemed ready to eat. If I so much as looked at food it seemed to take residence on my hips. I had rationalized my *sturdiness* by telling myself that men preferred ladies with more to *enjoy*. Truly, it had never hindered me in all my years. I had always had more than a sufficient number of male suitors who apparently appreciated *sturdiness* over thin and boney gals. It was more likely they thought I could work harder, and that I could bear children more easily, if truth be told.

The girls waded back to the bank and headed towards the blankets and baskets. Clumps of clouds brought shade to the open areas as we sat cooled under a grand sycamore. Once our bellies were full, we all leaned back on the blankets. Amos shut his eyes, and his mouth fell open. The girls and I pointed and giggled softly at this sight. Constance was already dozing and making her soft puffing sounds. Lila and Grace got up and decided to walk around the area to pick some wildflowers. I rested on my back and watched the clouds as I thought about the possibility of a second chance with Parker. My mind reviewed the images of the old gypsy woman and what she had said. I thought of the ghostly fortune teller and all the PBs. I thought of my handsome Parker on the train. I thought deeply about his parting whispers and his parting kiss. Love *is* ageless. Feeling it now, at my age, it was an even sweeter place to be. I reached to touch the small cross on my necklace. I realized that things do sometimes happen in mys-teri-ous ways, indeed.

Chapter 10

The next two days in Raleigh brought us time in the garden with Grace and Lila, more family dinners, a night at the theater with Amos, and several wanders to town again. These were days where my mind seemed agitated somehow. It churned with thoughts about my life and decisions that I had made in the past. The regrets seemed to grow. I felt the need to write these thoughts down, so I was journaling more besides the normal bedtime writings. Constance worked on her bag of stitch projects. She mentioned that one needed to be completed before Friday, because it was part of her graduation gift for Miss Grace. It was most enjoyable just to feel part of the normal family day without a lot of fanfare directed at us. When provided with a comfy rocker and a welcoming porch, I was always a good one for sitting and whiling away hours in thought. The cats seemed pleased that they had someone to sit outside with them. Both Constance and I had ventured into the study and found books we wanted to read. When our hands were not busy, our minds escaped to the writings of Thoreau, Whitman, and Emerson.

By Thursday evening, I felt on edge with no real explanation for it. Tomorrow was going to be busy day for the whole family. Constance and I excused ourselves and retired to bed early. We did our regular nightly rituals and went to bed without much conversation. Constance always seemed to easily drift into sleep, but I was not always so fortunate.

I did not sleep as I had hoped. I turned and twisted in the bed for hours. My mind would not calm. I occasionally looked out the window and checked the movement of the stars and constellations. I knew midnight was near when Cassiopeia showed itself to the middle of my window pane. I need to sleep. I need to sleep. So much to do for graduation day. I need…to…

Then the wind began. The wind is strong on my face. The trees are bowing and bending to its strength. I have got to get home. I have always been able to find my way. I do not even know how I got on this road. What road is this? I feel sacred and unsteady. I don't know what is down this road, and I wish I was not alone now. Confusion. I am going to go back the other way. I think that is safer. Yes, safer.

I turn to go the other direction. The road becomes a large iron bridge. I am lost. I am utterly lost. I do not know this place. I do not know what to do. I want to cry but I cannot. I stand frightened and unmoving like a baby deer. The wind continues to whip and tear at my dress and my hair. I have got to decide which way to go because the darkness is almost upon me. I look at the bridge but cannot determine what lies on the other side. I look at the wild and violent water of the river that lies beneath the bridge, and it too instills fear in me. When I look up again, I see my father at the other end of the bridge. He does not speak, yet I hear him telling me to go the other way and not use the bridge. I yell for him, but no sound comes from my throat. I try repeatedly to go towards him, but I cannot move. Without uttering any words, I hear him tell me again to go the other way. Somehow, I know he will watch over me. He will keep me safe.

I turn and stop. I stand looking down the darkening road, but now it does not frighten me so much. The stones in the road appear to glow with an amber color and it feels good to stand on it. Father understood. He was right. I wish he was near. The fear is lessening inside me. This feels like the right direction now. The wind still pushes at me and blowing leaves are striking me in the face as I step to move forward.

"Celia, wake up! Wake up!" Constance says, as she gently smacks my face to awaken me.

My eyes open to see the glow of the oil lamp. I am startled to see Constance sitting on the edge of my bed. I push her hands away from my face. "What in hell are you doing, Constance?"

"I was trying to bring you out of a bad dream. You were moaning and almost crying. You were turning back and forth in your bed like a demon was inside of you. Mercy! You were certainly thrashing about."

103

She poured a glass of water and offered it to me. "Here, Celia, take a sip of water. Are you ok now?"

I drank the water. "Yes, yes, and thank you. Go on back to bed. I am alright now. I am sorry I woke you."

"Oh hush, now. Let's both get back to some good dreams, ok? I am here if you need me."

"Good night, Constance. You always make things better." Sleep came to both of us and thankfully the dream did not return.

Friday morning arrived with rays of sunshine pouring into the east windows. All the family seemed to be buzzing about. Lila sang as she made coffee and put out muffins for breakfast. Grace was studying her piano music that she would play today. Amos was busy shaving and readying himself to be the proud father of a graduate. A feeling of happiness occupied the house as Constance and I enjoyed a few quiet moments of morning on the porch. The two cats were in usual attendance. I yawned, then Constance yawned, and when the cats followed suit, we laughed.

I breathed in the morning air deep into my lungs and let it out slowly. "It is going to be a good day," I said, as I raised my coffee cup in her direction.

"Yes, indeed. A good day for sure," Constance said. She gave a polite raise of her coffee cup in a like manner.

We sat quietly sipping our coffee and listening to the birds. Each cat took a turn getting up and moving into the spray of sunshine on the porch floor. They each lay down and stretched out as if to make sure the sun touched every inch of their body. For them, the day was starting in good fashion too.

When the old clock in the hall struck ten thirty, Amos announced it was time to leave. We all walked together towards the nursing college, where it sat impressively on Washington Street. As we promenaded the sidewalks of the town, Amos waved or spoke briefly to those he knew. We arrived on the college campus and made our way to the front entrance of the school. It seemed as if the parents of the graduates all wore an extra big smile of pride as they searched to find a good seat. Amos was beaming. He was also breaking into a sweat due to wearing his Sunday best and making the walk on this sultry morning. While he surveyed the crowd, he used his handkerchief to wipe his brow. Then he claimed his seat.

Graduation day for Grace was finally here. Her training had been arduous. Some of the young ladies had dropped out early on, or they had been asked to leave because they had been deemed unsuitable. The only applicants that were accepted were considered to have had a superior education. There were only eight in the graduating class. The head nurse had declared that Grace was one of the brightest and most focused of the all the young ladies. Amos and the rest of us grinned with pride as Grace entered the room with her classmates. She then moved to the piano, located near the stage, and sat down at it.

There was not a seat left unfilled in the warm and stuffy auditorium. Grace began to play the piano for the opening moments of the ceremony. She played flawlessly. When she finished, everyone was asked to stand for a prayer by Dean Horner. Upon the murmur of amens from the crowd, everyone sat again and awaited the address from Dr. Marshall Potts. Since I had not slept well last night, I caught myself nodding off a couple of times, as the doctor talked of dedication and compassion, et cetera. Constance nudged me on both occasions. She glared at me with a scowl each time. I was thankful that neither Amos nor Lila had witnessed my head bobs. Grace was up front, so she could not have seen me either. I brought out my fan thinking that would help me stay awake, and it did.

After Dr. Potts finished his address, there was a vocal solo by Harriett Beal, one of the members of the graduating class. She was not horrible, but I thought she was not that talented either. I remembered Amos telling me that the Beal family had a lot of influence in the town. No doubt, they had *influenced* someone to allow their daughter to perform, despite her vocal limitations. I almost felt sorry for the girl, but decided it was us, the audience, which needed that sentiment. Once Harriett finished, it came time for each graduate to receive their diploma. This was followed by brief prayer as a close to the ceremony. Someone else played the piano as the procession of new nurses filed out of the auditorium. Each one collected their nurse's cap as they passed the stage, and the audience clapped until the last graduate had left the room.

Families gathered immediately outside on the college grounds to congratulate and embrace the new nurses. Once Constance and I had praised and hugged Grace, we found a bench near a shade tree on which to sit. We decided to wait on the bench and simply observe the celebrations of all the families until Amos and the girls were ready to leave.

"This is a grand day for the Broadmore family, Celia," said Constance. "A very special day."

I nodded with tears beginning to well in my eyes while attempting to retrieve a handkerchief from my purse. "I am so happy that I could be here to see this and be part of their celebration. I just love them all so much. And you are the cherry on top, Miss Constance. I am so grateful you could join me in my travels, and that we could share such a good time together."

"Now do not start getting all sappy on me, or we will both be sitting here crying and blowing our noses. That would not be a pretty sight. Besides, you are not so *dainty* when it comes to clearing your nose." That statement made us both laugh, as we leaned into each other slightly, our shoulders touching. The humor helped to stop the tears.

"Alright, alright. Enough sappiness for now," I said. "We only have today with the family, and then we will be back on the train. The days have gone fast, don't you think?"

"They sure have. We are going cook your family a fine celebration meal. And we will have us one heck of a good time this afternoon. Amos even said he would break out his fiddle! I might be *persuaded* to play the spoons. If we drink us some bourbon, you won't even have to ask me. I'll be primed and ready!"

Then I heard Lila call my name from behind the bench. "Auntie Celia! Auntie Celia!" As I turned to look in her direction, I heard a squeak from Constance, and then she cleared her throat as a signal to me. Lord o' mercy! Lila had brought Chief Bordeaux to us.

"Auntie, look who I found in the crowd?" Lila grinned with her announcement.

"Well, we just keep bumping into each other, don't we now? This is another delightful surprise," I said, while thinking the total opposite. The chief nodded and said hello to Constance and myself.

"Chief Bordeaux, did you have a daughter graduating today too?" Constance asked.

"No, no. My niece, Harriett Beal, is why I am here today. And of course, I do know Grace, as well," he replied. "I am sure you are as proud as I am to see these outstanding young ladies take on the demanding career of nursing."

Constance and I both agreed most earnestly. Lila was still standing nearby. She spoke up to invite Chief Bordeaux to join us for our celebration. Constance cleared her throat again.

"Yes, that is a kind and gracious offer, but I have already committed to attending the party for my niece, so I will have to decline."

"Well, maybe you can come by just for dessert later in the day, if you like," Lila continued. For Pete's sake, I thought, was Lila trying to play matchmaker? She seemed so insistent that the chief join us. "I am sure Daddy would enjoy some conversation with you too. He never says it, but I think he gets a bit tired of only women to converse with at home."

"Dessert sounds lovely. I just may be able to make that happen. Thank you, Lila. Thank you, ladies." The chief smiled, nodded, and gave us a little wink. He excused himself to rejoin his sister and her family on the lawn. Lila returned to the crowd too to find her father and sister.

Before Constance could utter a sound, I spun and said to her, "Don't you say a thing." Constance managed to contain herself by slightly biting her lower lip. Her face frowned too. "Let's go see if the family is ready to leave. You and I still have a lot to prepare for the meal." I stood up, and Constance followed. I was amazed she had kept quiet upon command. That had *never* happened before. I smiled to myself and grabbed to take her hand. "It's ok to talk now, just don't mention Chief P.B., the gypsy, the fortuneteller, or Parker. Today is all about Grace and the family, and I do not want to hear anything about all that other silliness."

Constance squeezed my hand a little and then said, "Yes, mother Celia. I'll be good." And we laughed while swinging our clasped hands back and forth like young school girls.

Chapter 11

As Constance and I scuttled and busied about the kitchen preparing the meal, I kept thinking about Parker. I'm not sure why he was on my mind, with all we had to complete, but he was. I had not revealed to Constance that maybe I was beginning to change my thoughts about the idea of rekindling my relationship with him. We had not talked of him since our arrival in Raleigh. He had implied that he wanted reconciliation. I felt there was no doubt about the meaning of what he had whispered to me. If I did bring myself to tell Constance, I had better be covering my ears, or wearing ear plugs, as I could only imagined her shrieks of joy. She had not minced words in the past about how asinine my behavior was in not accepting his marriage proposal. She had even encouraged me to swallow my pride and go after him. Sometimes I think she understood me better than I did. True friends told you the truth, even when it was not easy to hear, or easy for them to say. I loved her dearly for that.

"Celia, did you hear me?" Constance said bringing me back into the moment.

Clearing my head of Parker thoughts, I turned towards her. "What is it?"

"You act as if you mind is somewhere else. Are you feeling ok?"

"I'm good. I'm just fine. I want everything we fix to be perfect. Remind me to pick some flowers from the garden for the table, will you?"

"Will do," said Constance. She shrugged off my change of subject, but it left a question in her mind.

"I think my bread pudding is ready for the oven now." I opened the oven door for her, and she slid the large pan inside. She flipped the dish towel over her shoulder, turned, paused, and then pointed to the counter. She began to set the ingredients for her next project from the counter onto the kitchen table, where she would have more room to work. She claimed I was cramping her style, and she needed more elbow room.

I continued with cleaning the chicken and preparing it for the oven. I made the pea salad, marinated some sliced cucumbers, and then peeled potatoes. Constance was now mixing the batter for the corn dodgers that Amos had requested, while her famous bread pudding continued to bake. Her bread pudding was like ambrosia of the gods. It took all my will power not to take a big bite once it sat to cool.

On the trip to town yesterday, Constance and I procured something special for our meal; fresh lemons for lemonade. I smiled as I cut the lemons and squeezed the juices into the pitcher. It seemed that lemons were the perfect thing to rub and smell when you have the blues. I didn't really have the blues, but I was experiencing a uniqueness inside me that I could not quite put a name on. The lemon smell and taste had somehow lifted my spirits. I was pleased to offer the surprise of fresh lemonade. I imagined when the others smelled it that they would all break into smiles too.

Amos was reading the paper on the front porch while twirling a toothpick in his mouth. When I periodically glanced his way through the kitchen window, I sometimes caught him dozing a bit. It was good seeing him relaxed and resting. Since they were not preparing the meal today, the girls had made plans to stop by a house of a friend or two on the way home. The two cats sat quietly on the porch near Amos. They stared at the screen door to the kitchen as if willing us with their minds to feed them something. I made a mental note to myself to save some chicken scraps for them. Constance hummed and whistled to herself as she worked. This was a happy day in so many ways. I hated that we would have to leave tomorrow.

By one thirty lunch was ready and the table set, and everyone was gathered. Constance and I received applause and compliments from Amos and the girls on the smells and the display of food. "Besides our bellies, the eyes must eat too," said Constance, as she placed the last dish on the table.

"You have most certainly accomplished that, ladies. Mmmm, mmmm! It all looks so wonderful!" Amos said. We all sat and bowed our heads.

My nephew gave thanks, and the clinking of forks on our plates was the only sound for several minutes. In the rush to get to graduation, breakfast had not consisted of much. We all appeared to be starving as we ate without talking. I finally paused and reminded everyone to save room for the bread pudding, as it was not to be missed.

"You do not have to remind me," Amos said. "I have never forgotten how good it always is, and I would crawl if I had to in order to get some."

"Oh, Amos!" Constance said chuckling. "You can thank my great granny, Opal, for it. It is her recipe." Without planning it, we all shouted in unison, "Thank you, Granny Opal!" This was followed by a burst of laughter at the shared coincidence.

Once our bellies could hold no more, and the conversation had lagged, Constance and I shooed everyone outdoors. We were determined to cook and clean up today. It was our way of saying thank you to my family and to help with the celebration. Constance took care of the leftovers, and I scraped and stacked the dishes and pots for washing. I watched again through the kitchen window as Amos lit a cigar, and Lila and Grace set up the domino game.

I washed and Constance dried. As I the scrubbed and swirled the plates and pots in the murky water, my mind wandered again to Parker. Constance recognized I was not listening to her again. "For Pete's sake, Celia. Hello! Where are you? Are you sure you are alright today? You can't seem to stay focused. Where is your mind going?"

"Sorry. I'm really quite fine. I need to share something with you."

"Spill it, sister. What exactly is going on in the noggin' of yours?" Constance asked as she leaned against the counter, folded her arms, and waited.

I looked at Constance. "Am I too old?" I asked.

"What? Hell yes, you're old! That's no revelation," she said in her normal teasing tone. "Too old? What do you mean, too old? Too old for what?"

I sighed and put down my rag and looked Constance in the eyes. "You know, on second thought, this is not the time and place for this conversation. We will be on the train tomorrow, and we will have privacy and more than enough time to talk. I will tell you then. I promise. Let's just wait until we are on the train. Ok?"

"Alright then. I know you will keep your word. How about we go upstairs and get our gifts for Grace and join the others on the porch?" I agreed. I appreciated how Constance always knew when to just leave me be.

We returned to the porch and presented our gifts. Constance was skilled in the art of making fine lace doilies. She presented Grace with two beautiful large ones tied with a satin bow. Grace embraced Constance and thanked her profusely. Lila gave her sister a silk scarf that she had instructed Samuel to purchase when he was in

Washington, D.C. on a previous trip. Grace pulled the scarf through the air as if to dance with it, and then she wrapped it about her neck. She kissed her sister and praised the beauty of Lila's gift. I had brought Grace a pair of earrings that had belonged to my mother. These were earrings that I adored as a child and rarely allowed to touch. They were crescent-shaped earrings with a single pearl perched on the inside of each crescent. I always thought they looked like dangly little slivers of moons. I had loved them and truly enjoyed wearing them. I had remembered Grace doting on them on my last visit, and I thought they would be perfect for her gift. Needless to say, she was thrilled and put them on immediately. Her beaming smile affirmed that I had chosen the right gift. Amos slipped away and brought out a large gift wrapped in one of Lila's shawls. It turned out to be a lap dulcimer. It was something he knew Grace had been wanting for some time. She was beside herself and overjoyed with his gift. She hugged and kissed her daddy like when she was a little girl on Christmas morning.

"Hello there!" came an unexpected shout from a man on the street. We all turned to see that it was Chief Bordeaux approaching the steps of the porch. He removed his hat and bid us all good evening. "I thought I would take Lila up on her offer of dessert and share in the celebration today," he said.

My muscles tightened. I got the usual nudge from Constance too. I hoped no one noticed. I was sure she was smirking, but I dared not look at her.

I had been hopeful that I would not have to have a dalliance with the chief this evening. He was a perfectly decent man and pleasant to the eye, but I was not interested. Nor was I in the mood to entertain any gentlemen callers. Tonight, I was tired and my thoughts were elsewhere. I would, of course, do my best to be social and not embarrass my family.

Amos spoke up, "We were just about to go inside for dessert. Your timing is perfect, sir. Good to see you, Percy," Amos said. He patted the chief on his back, as they entered the house.

"Same here, Amos. It is always a pleasure."

The bread pudding delighted everyone, and Constance even went back for seconds. We ladies cleared the table and then went out to the porch to join the men. The cool breeze of the evening made the porch the best location for conversation. The talk varied from today's graduation, to business, to updates on the progress of the library plans that Amos was working on. Surprisingly, I mostly sat and rocked and just listened. We all remarked about the almost full moon tonight, and because of its brightness, we had no need for candles or oil lamps. The moonlight bathed everything in the yard with an exceptional glow. I noticed how the calico cat sat in the moonlight as if it were bathing in sunshine.

With little encouragement needed, Amos played his fiddle for us. He tuned it and then made it sing. We all sang along on some of the songs like Silver

117

Threads Among the Gold and Liza Jane. With toes tapping and hands clapping, the music was the perfect end to this day of celebration. I hoped it would wind down soon. I stifled a yawn.

Without warning, Percy stood and looked straight at me. "Miss Celia, would like to accompany me on a short walk to the garden? We won't be gone long. I know the evening is getting late, and you have had a tiring day. It would be a pleasure if you would join me. I think the flowers will be a beautiful sight in the moonlight."

While I smiled on the outside, I cringed on the inside. I stood and said, "Sounds absolutely lovely." Constance cleared her throat in the background. Percy presented his hand to assist me down the steps. Once on the ground, he placed my arm through his, and we began our stroll to the back of the house where both the flower and vegetable gardens were located.

He was right. The flowers had a unique brilliance in the moonlight. All the plants took on an exceptional appearance when bathed in the moon's glow. The captain kept a firm but polite hold on my arm as we stood and looked at the garden. "I hear you are leaving tomorrow. I regret that you and Miss Constance are not staying longer. It would have been my pleasure to have taken you both to dinner, or perhaps another day in the country. Let me just say, I wish I could have gotten to know you better, Miss Celia. I think you are such a delight and a remarkable beauty."

"My goodness, Chief Bordeaux, that is so kind of you to say. I had no idea these thoughts were in your head." While my words were polite, my mind was twitching. I stepped back and released my arm from his, but he still gently held my hand. We now looked at each other straight on.

"Please, call me Percy," he said. I smiled and nodded, and I patted his hand that held mine.

"You know, Percy, I believe things happen for a reason. And for some reason we are not meant to be together, for I live in another city, and I must return home. I love Augusta, and it will always be my home. I don't travel to Raleigh often, and at my age, I do not even know if the good Lord will allow me to wake the next day. Let's just say, if it were a different time in my life, I would be floating on clouds with what you just said to me. I will pray that you meet someone who will bring joy into your life and love you as you should be loved. You are a quality man with handsome features. I am surprised you don't have all the single, older women in town baking pies for you!" I was relieved when Percy laughed at this.

"I understand, Miss Celia. I saw a sparkle in your eyes that I could not ignore, so I felt I needed to speak my mind before you left, just in case there was a chance. I will take your prayers and hope for the best," he said smiling. "Let's get you back on the porch, and then I will make my way home."

Once Percy had left, I found Constance and declared that I needed a stiff drink. "I'll take care of that," Constance said, as she turned to go to the kitchen. She knew where the spirits were kept. Amos politely excused himself and said he felt ready for bed. Lila and Grace had already gone upstairs to read before they retired. Constance returned with two small glasses of bourbon, and we sat down at the dining room table. We touched our glasses together as we always did, and then we chugged our whiskey in one gulp.

"You know I want to know what went on in the garden," Constance said, while looking straight ahead and avoiding eye contact with me.

"I'm ready for bed. How about you?"

"Right behind you," she answered. She picked up the glasses, returned them to the kitchen, and padded up the stairs behind me.

We changed into our night clothes and washed our faces. We combed our hair in silence. Constance climbed into bed without doing any stitching, claiming her eyes were already shut, and she wanted to go right to sleep. She intuitively knew I still did not want to talk. I announced that I had to write a few things in my journal, and I would be not far behind.

I opened my journal to a new page and began to write.

Do I take a leap of faith? I am scared. I want to be free of the guilt. I am tired of its burden. Do I deserve love? Nathan, forgive me. Parker, my heart has always been yours.

I closed my journal and turned out the lamp. The bed felt comforting to my tired bones. I reminded myself that I could not predict the future. As I lay in the dark, I silently prayed for what was in my heart. I wanted exactly what Constance and Vernon had with each other all these years. I wanted to be loved until I died and beyond. I had always wanted it. After what had happened to Nathan, I believed that I did not deserve happiness. I wanted to let that weight go now and to love unconditionally. I dearly wanted Parker in my life again. "Please Lord," I begged out loud, and then I drifted into sleep.

Christine Bradfield

122

Chapter 12

The time in Raleigh had gone too fast. We stood at the train station now, saying our goodbyes and expressing gratitude to Amos and his family. The train was ready to leave in a matter of minutes. I hugged each of them repeatedly. It was even harder to leave this time. Because of my age, I was unsure if my health would hold to allow me a return visit. My nose was now running because my tears were coming. I already saw Constance wipe some tears. We were a soggy, sappy mess, but I did not care. I made Amos and his girls promise to come for a visit to Augusta in the not-too-distant future, so I could show them the city and all it offered. It probably annoyed him, but I made him pinky swear to it in front of all the people on the train platform. One last hug as the train whistle blew and the porter announced, "All aboard!"

Luckily, we had seats on the platform side of the train, and we waved until their faces were out of sight. As we sat and watched the city fade away, Constance squeezed my hand, and we both dabbed at tears. She assured me I would be back to visit again, and that maybe the visit would be to see a new addition to the family, or to see Grace get married.

"Get the bottle, I am in need of a sip or two…or more," Constance said in a quiet voice.

"Oh, hell yes, me too," I said not so delicately. A woman older than us, who was sitting across the aisle, gave us a sideways glance that reeked of judgement. I gave her a sugary smile and moved the bottle in her direction, as if to offer her a nip. She looked horrified and instantly turned away. I guess that took care of her. I was in a mood and not acting too ladylike at the moment.

I took a sip of the bourbon, leaned my head back, and let it slide down my throat slowly. I felt unsettled. So many unexplainable things had happened on this trip. I don't know why I was trying to give credibility to the fortune teller and the gypsy. I laughed to myself. And where was Parker? Was he living in Charlotte? Was he there visiting someone? Was his stop business related? Did he have a family? Was he a widower? It dawned on me, like a thump on the head, that I knew nothing about his life now. Our conversation had been so brief. I came out of these thoughts when I felt Constance pat my arm.

"Boy, oh boy, you looked deep in thought just now. Want me to leave you alone?"

"No, I just needed a moment. I'm good. It is always hard to leave, especially when there is such a distance between you and those you love. Did I mention how glad I am that you came with me?" Constance smiled, nodded, and patted my arm again. "You are my sunshine, Constance," I said as

I passed her the bottle. "Your friendship is one my greatest gifts."

"Likewise, Celia, I feel the same about you. I cannot imagine anyone but crazy, outrageous, old you as my best friend. But I can only take so much mushy stuff for one day. Now let's get on to the real talk you promised me."

I really felt like napping between the bourbon and the sway of the train, but I began to talk. I took a deep breath and exhaled slowly. "I've lied to you for years." Constance's eyes widened and then narrowed a bit as she turned to look at me. Amazingly, she did not let out a peep. "It is not what you think. And God help me, I am going to admit you were right. I loved Parker. Hell, I still love Parker. I have always loved him. I pushed the ache of love down deep and tried to quiet it. I should have gone after him, just like you told me. You were also right when you said I pushed love away. I did. Parker was as close to perfect as I would ever find in a man after losing my dear Nathan. You know I blamed myself because he died. I am not sure I will ever stop blaming myself for Nathan's death." Constance listened and stayed silent. She stared out the window as I talked. She took a sip and returned the bottle to my hand.

"You saw how Parker acted, and you know what he said to me. Is it too late? Am I too old for love now? I always felt love had no age. I think we all want love no matter where we are in life. I want what you and Vernon have. I don't want to be alone anymore. I have experienced all the *variety* that I needed in life a long time ago. I want to find Parker and see if there is still a chance for us, before I am stone cold in the ground."

Constance looked remarkably unmoved by my admission. She leaned to take out her stitchwork. I thought that this was a sign that she needed more calming than the bourbon had offered her. She still had not uttered a word about the bombshell that I had just dropped. I waited a few moments. I was perplexed that she did not immediately respond.

"Constance, aren't you going to say something?" I asked. I was still surprised by her silence.

"I don't need to *say* anything. You have *fi-nal-ly* figured it out, Celia," she said with dripping sarcasm. "Good lord, how I wished you had come to this conclusion, oh, let's say…forty years ago!" We were face to face when she said this. We both broke into loud laughter. The old lady next to us grimaced in disgust at our outburst. I could not stop heehawing. Constance always told it like it was and pulled no punches. She was good for my soul.

"I guess your ears were plugged shut back then, and your brain wandered off too," Constance added. "I did my best to talk sense into you all these years. Back then I think your *zestfulness* interfered with your brain function. That is usually a man problem, but it seemed to affect you too!" Our laughter lasted until our stomachs hurt. Every head in the train car had turned to determine where the cackling was coming from. I felt renewed. I felt calmer after sharing it all with Constance. Now I just had to figure out how to find Parker. I stowed the almost empty bottle back in my parcel. Our stomachs were calling for food.

We moved to the dining car and placed our order. It seemed that everyone within earshot of the obese, greasy-haired salesman was annoyed by the fact that he would not shut his pie hole. He rambled on loudly about his travels. I am not even sure he was talking to anyone in particular. Constance shot me a glance that said do not start any trouble. A crash of glassware caused a brief silence in the dining car. When I leaned to see what happened, I saw the backside of a man's head and had a fainting moment of thinking it was Parker. It was not. I needed to get a grip on myself. Everything in due time. But when you are my age, you want to speed up the results. We ate our bland food and reminisced about the wonderful gifts that Grace received for her graduation. Once we finished eating, we agreed to retire early to our sleeping car.

As Constance stitched, I could almost feel her desire to get back home. She loved to travel, but she never wanted to be gone too long from Vernon, her children, and most especially her grandchildren. Seven days was a long time in her mind.

"I bet Vernon will be glad to have you back home," I said. I watched as she smiled without

127

looking up. "And those grandkids are going to squeal and climb all over you!"

"I miss that old buzzard. He can't cook at all, so I hope my girls stopped by and brought him food, or did some cooking at the house for him. I admit, it was hard to sleep at times without him next to me. I do not think we have ever been apart this long since we were married. And I started missing those little ones the moment we left the train station in Augusta. I am simple that way. Those grandkids can work me like a puppet, but never let them know that. They will love the candy I bought for them. I will just have to stop them from eating it all at once."

"You are blessed, Constance, and so is your family, because they have you." She smiled again without looking up from her work. On that note, I pulled out my journal and began to write notes about how I would try to go about tracking down Parker. It might take a while, but I was sure I could get it accomplished. The sway of the car rocked me to sleep with my pen still in my hand. Constance gently placed a blanket over me after taking the pen and closing the journal, placing them back in my bag. She readied her bed and crawled in. I was exhausted. I slept in that same position all night. I was awakened by the train whistle at dawn.

It was Sunday morning now, and Constance warned me about my colorful storytelling. "Mind your manners, Celia," she said. "This is God's day and I do not feel like turning to stone."

"It is entirely your fault that I tell such stories and share my *unconventional* thoughts with you. You are my best audience. You always laugh and that is what makes me spout more, and show my ass more!"

"You are so shameful, Celia. I have to laugh or I will bust," Constance admitted. "I have lost hope that you will *ever* change. I should receive sainthood for loving you as you are; a heathen so full of *zest*." And with that comment, our laughter was off and running with the sunrise.

In a few hours we would be back home. I was thankful for my home and now I almost ached for it. I needed more time to understand all that was going on inside me now. I felt the necessity for an extended rest before beginning the task of locating Parker. I could not wait to sleep again in my own bed.

Constance nudged me from my thoughts and pulled me to my feet, so that we could get breakfast. Her stomach growled next to my ear as I stood. What she I both wanted most was coffee and a sweet roll. Between the sips and nibbles, Constance complained that she had not slept well. As we waited to be served, I whined that my neck felt stiff and sore. I reminded her that we would be home in our own beds tonight and probably sleep like babies.

When the train pulled into the station, Vernon quietly and patiently waited by the side of the platform away from all the other people. He had brought their buggy to take us home. I found out later that he had arrived an hour early. He had missed his Constance that was a given. He raised one hand in an attempt to wave as the train pulled in. "There's the old, crusty buzzard now," Constance said, as she waved to Vernon from our window. We checked to make sure we had all our belongings. We waited until the train completely stopped before moving towards the doors. Constance' words echoed in my brain, and I remembered to grab the handrail as I exited the train and made my way down the steps. I did not need a repeat performance of my landing in Raleigh.

Vernon moved through the crowd to greet us. He did not show public affection often. But on this day, he kissed Constance on the cheek and embraced her tightly, before grabbing our bags. Her eyes widened at the unusually amorous greeting Vernon gave her, and this time, it was I that gave *her* a little bump with my elbow. She winked and laughed. Without words shared, we both had the same thought; it is good to be home.

We mostly road in silence until reaching my house, where the buggy stopped with a jerk and a slight roll. I leaned to hug and kiss Constance, and I said we would talk soon over tea. Vernon took my hand and helped me from the wagon. He set my bags on the porch as I requested. I teared up again as Constance twisted in her seat to wave as the buggy rolled east. At last glance, Vernon had placed his arm around his bride. It melted my heart to see this.

I stood there a moment. I looked around the property and inhaled the air. My hired hand, Delby, had Sunday off, so I would have the place to myself today. I had a heaviness hanging on me even though I was pleased to be home. I decided I would sit and watch the sunset this evening, and let my favorite tea calm me before bed. Hopefully, I would wake refreshed tomorrow with a renewed spirit.

Chapter 13

After an extended trip, it was always a relief of sorts to return to the familiarity and comfort of one's own home. Home meant sanctuary and solace to me. I had come to love time alone after years of practice. Although I had thoroughly enjoyed my days with Constance and my family, I felt the need to be comforted. I ached for my own bed as a refuge.

As I walked up to the house, I judged the condition of my rose bushes. To my delight they were loaded with deep red blooms. It was then I realized why I was feeling a sort of sadness inside myself. It had nothing to do with the trip coming to an end and not having Constance around. Every year as June first came near, I got the sadness. It was a bit less year by year, but it still came. It always partnered with the guilt. A guilt I carried all my life since the day I learned Nathan had died. I guess the trip had occupied my mind enough that it had not come to the forefront until now. Another year had passed, and it was time to visit him again. I dutifully went every year to take him one of my roses, talk for a while, and leave him with a kiss. The first day of June arrived tomorrow.

I slowly climbed the steps and entered the house. I felt tired and wanted to drop everything right at the door. Instead, I pushed on to take my things into the bedroom. For now, I flopped the suitcase and small parcels on the bed. I promised myself I would deal with them later. I made my way to the kitchen and fixed my favorite tea. Staring out the window as the wood burned and the water heated, I wondered how many years was it now? I should have easily remembered, but I had to make the calculation again. Forty-seven years he had been gone from my touch. Forty-seven years I had blamed myself for my carelessness that had caused it all. I sighed. I fixed my tea and walked outside to the porch. The sun was moving low. I loved sitting in the dim light of dusk, but today I was weary and uneasy. I sat in my rocker and sipped on the tea until it was cold. I stood and I tossed what was left of the tea off the side of the porch. It was not quite dark, but I decided to go to bed anyway.

During the night I fought to sleep. I could not stop the flickers of memories of the day that Nathan died. It was my fault. I had not properly latched the cattle pen gate and two of the cows had gotten out. I saw the image again of Nathan saddling up to go round up the strays. In the limbo of sleep and not sleep, I screamed and sat up when I saw the dream face of Emery, Nathan's best friend. My nightgown was stuck to me with sweat. Emery was the one who had to tell me that Nathan was dead, apparently thrown from his horse, and his head hit the rocks. I grabbed at my head wanting these thoughts to clear. "I am so sorry, Nathan. I'm so sorry," I whispered to his spirit. I cried until I slept.

When morning came, I prepared for the walk and my visit with Nathan. Feeling drained of all my strength, I was slower than normal in getting ready this morning. I selected a light-weight dress and plucked my big brimmed straw hat from the top shelf of my wardrobe. I would need the shade of the hat during my walk. I always preferred to walk there. I might get a bit warm on the walk, but once there I would be shaded while I visited. Everything there would be shaded by the splendid old oak that stood grandly near the cemetery entrance. Noting how hot it already was so early in the morning, I packed a jar of sweet tea. The last thing to do before leaving was to cut the prettiest rose from one of the bushes and wrap it in my handkerchief to take with me.

By eleven, I started out the door and on my way. The sun in summer fashion was bright and hot on my shoulders. I scolded myself for not getting an earlier start since it would have been much cooler then. Not far into my walk, I could smell new-cut hay in the air. I loved the smells of nature and the earth, and I always paid particular attention to them. Maybe not so much on this morning, though. This year the walk felt a bit different, but I was not sure exactly why. Maybe because I was so much older, and only the Lord knew how much longer I would be able to do this. I had once confessed to Constance that I often prayed that when I died that

I would meet up with Nathan in the next life. That he would be there lovingly waiting to bring me into the next world, and that I would see all those I had loved gathered with him. I smiled at the thought of seeing his face again. When I had that picture in my mind the fear of death did not exist.

I was there before I realized it. The church was coming into view now. I walked behind the church to the cemetery gate and paused in the shade of my favorite oak to try to cool myself. I was thankful for a slight breeze at that very moment. I carefully unwrapped the rose then used my hanky to wipe the sweat under my eyes and on my brow. On I walked to his grave. I sat down next to the stone and leaned back against it. I took off my hat and laid it upside down, and I set my jar of tea inside it. To my surprise I noticed a Cooper's hawk sitting in the oak tree. I felt as if it was staring at me. I remembered seeing it here before on several occasions. The mighty oak was a perfect place to oversee much of the area. It was no wonder the hawk sought to land there.

My mind was rolling with thoughts while I listened to the bees, the bugs, the birds, and watched the hawk. I had thoughts of Nathan, loss, death, my own death, and even thoughts of Parker of all things. I sat in silence for several minutes. I loved the exquisite silence that only a cemetery can provide. I always found it to be soothing. But today my thoughts and memories were causing me nervousness. My thoughts were almost making me

136

feel a little out of control. I shook my head wanting my mind to clear to the present moment, and it finally obliged me. There was something different I needed to say to Nathan this year. It was what was causing the heaviness over me.

"Nathan, I love you. Always will. You know that the Lord only knows how many more visits I will be able to make, but rest assured, I'll come each year if I can." I went on to tell him that some surprisingly strange things had happened recently on my trip out east. Things that put my mind in a whirl, but also brought other thoughts into focus. I said my mind had somehow started processing things I had pushed way to the back and had not wanted to deal with until now. It was like I had no control, like something inside myself was telling me that I had to face certain facts before I die. I told him I had made a decision about something, and I hoped he would understand.

"You see, the thing is, Nathan, I'm old. I am an old woman, and my life is getting shorter by the minute. And I am tired. I am tired, and I have to let go of some heavy weight in my heart to keep on going. I fear I have only been half living all these years, pretending my life was just how I wanted it. I hope you will understand, Nathan, but I have to let go of the guilt of that day. I made the worst mistake of my life. I caused your death. But I cannot carry this guilt any longer. I have carried it these forty some years, and it hasn't made a difference, and it never will. You are still gone. I need to forgive myself, and I ask that you forgive me as well. I hope you can. My guilt will not bring you back. I truly wish I would have realized this years ago. I am sure my life would have been much different. After the mistake I made, I guess I felt that I did not deserve to be loved and to be happy. It was like the guilt was my punishment of sorts. I am done with the guilt now. I have to be done with it."

"And you know what else, Nathan? All these years I have been running scared of loving and losing someone again. I have pushed away every man that I started to have feelings for, even Parker. I think you would like him. He is a bona fide high-quality man. He's good in all ways. Besides you, he is the only other man of such fine quality that I ever thought I could marry. I sent him on his way too. I feared I would die if I loved again, and had to endure the type of grief that I had for you that took me to the dark, and wanted to keep me there. But I have decided I am willing to risk that now. Because for whatever reason, even being the sinner that I am, I have been given a second chance. I am actually going to start loving again, before it is too late. I pray you understand all this. It would nice if you could give me a sign of sorts, so I know that you do."

Again, I sat in silence for a few minutes more. I raised my hand to touch the cross on my necklace. I had one last thing to say. "Nathan, if when I die, and Satan does not get me first, I feel deeply that we will be together again. And when that happens, please wear your blue suit, Sweetheart. It was always my favorite. You always looked extra handsome in a suit." And with those words, I bent down, brushed the leaves from the base of the stone, and place the red rose next to it. I kissed my hand then touched my hand to his grave. "I'll be going now. I love you, always and ever."

I got up, put my hat on, and took a drink of tea. I thought, why did I bring tea? What I needed right now was a shot of bourbon. But tea would have to do. The hawk took flight from the oak and startled me a bit. I had forgotten that it was there. I headed home with less of a burden now than when I had arrived. Along the walk I noticed more of the summer flowers and various trees. My heart was lighter and my head more cleared. Apparently, the hawk was going the way with me, because every once in a while, he would fly past me and wait, and then repeat the process while continuing to move in the direction that I was headed. How unusual it seemed to me that the bird was doing this, but somehow it offered me comfort in a way. I made a mental note to add this to my journal the next time.

As I neared the house, I could see a man sitting on my porch, and it jolted me. I squinted as if that would help my vision, but I could not make out who it was exactly. I was not expecting anyone. It wasn't Delby because he had gone to help finish with the barn raising. He would not return until late day, if then. I stopped walking. Being cautious, I reached into my bag for my pistol, but I quickly realized that my fuzzy, morning brain had forgotten to retrieve the gun from my nightstand before leaving. I looked at him again. He is probably just a salesman, I hoped. But he sure had made himself right at home on my porch though, as if he lived there. The thought of having to deal with someone right now irritated me. I surely hoped he was not one of those sidewinders selling the next miracle elixir. Those kinds were so damn annoying. I sometimes bought something just so they would shut up and leave. Once again that darn hawk startled me as it flew past, circled in the air, and landed on the cottonwood tree on the north side of the house. It seemed content to sit there and observe.

The man noticed that I had stopped. He stood up and yelled, "Celia, honey, don't be scared. It's me, Parker," and then he turned and walked down the steps.

"Oh my, God! Good Lord! Parker! What on earth? What the…" I looked up to the sky and said, "Lord, you do work mysteriously sometimes and quite efficiently too, I might add."

Feeling flustered, nervous, and about ready to burst into tears, I finally got my feet to move, and I walked towards him. "Parker Boyd!" I said at almost a shout. "You have the damnedest way of appearing out of thin air!" He flashed a smile and I melted. We embraced each other tightly. Then we stepped apart to look at each other.

"I told you I would be seeing you again, Celia," he said with a wide grin. "You know I have my ways of finding out things. I also had no doubt you were still living in your daddy's house. Who would want to leave this beautiful place, on this gorgeous land?"

"I thought I was hallucinating when you said it was you." My goodness he looked good, I thought. It was hard to believe he was nearly seventy-one years old now.

"We have a lot to talk about. Come on up on the porch. I have some refreshment for us." He took my hand and up the steps we went. I let him lead me like a child.

I looked at the small porch table and on it were two of my little juice glasses, and setting next to them was a small bottle of bourbon. He saw that I was looking at the table and he said, "I remembered how you often liked a little nip in the afternoon." He gave me a wink. "Come on, let's sit, sip a little, and catch up." Parker never forgot anything, even the littlest of details. We sat. He poured us a nip. We touched our glasses together as if toasting, but we said nothing. I was overwhelmed to see him sitting right next to me. Tears welled in my eyes. We both sat and starred down the hill into the lushness of the valley.

He started to talk. "I missed you so terribly all these years. I am glad *divine intervention,* as you call it, has brought us back together. I think the Lord does have a plan for us, Celia. But he sure has taken his sweet time with it. We are really getting on in years. Old but not dead though," he said with

141

a laugh. "I still have friskiness in me at times." We both laughed and I knew he was trying to break the tension in the air. "Knowing you, you probably still have full supply of *zest* as well," and we chuckled again. His voice felt so reassuring to me, but I still could not get my head straight in the moment, too much emotion coming at me this day. And why all this in one day?

While I tried to form words to carry the conversation, I watched as Parker poured us a second shot of whiskey. I looked again at the view of the valley down the hill in front of us while gathering my composure. I took a deep breath and let it out slowly. "How long are you planning to stay in Augusta, Parker?" I finally uttered.

He turned to look at me. "Well, I guess that depends on you, Miss Celia. I could be quite content to sit on this porch each evening with you and watch every sunset for the rest of my life. How long would you like me to stay?"

Hearing what he just said, I was choked up with emotion, feeling like I could not squeeze out a single word. I was at a loss for something clever to say. Then I realized it was not a time to be clever and witty. It was time to be honest. I looked at his consuming, brown eyes and said, "Darling, I want you to stay forever, if you want." And with that remark, I reached for his hand and held it. He lifted my hand and kissed it then put his other hand on top of mine.

"Well, that's a good thing for my heart to hear. I have waited all my life for you, Celia. I never felt the call to be with any other woman. Oh, I have had companions, but I have not loved. You are the reason I have known love. You are my only love, Miss Celia. I was not sure this day would come, but I had prayed it would. Time and again, I prayed. I thought many times of coming back, but I was not sure you would have me. My pride and the thought of rejection, yet again, kept me from returning, until now. But after our meeting on the train, when I felt your heart, and saw what was in your eyes, I knew then I would come back, and as fast as I could get here. I am also glad to hear you want me to stay, because I already put my luggage in your bedroom", he said with a big smile and a wink. I smiled at hearing this, but I was still choking down emotion, and struggled not to cry streams of joyful tears.

Without the slightest clue of what was coming next in my brain I blurted out, "Parker, will you marry me?" I said without hesitation, surprising myself, and clearly surprising him. I saw his eyebrows rise up and his eyes get big. Without a reply, he stood up to move in front of my rocking chair. He bent to hold on to the arms of the chair, and then lowered himself to one knee. He took my hand again and said, "Celia, I would be honored to marry you. I knew the day would eventually get here when you would come to your senses." We both had tears about to fall. He kissed my hand, stood up, and pulled me up out of my chair and held me tight. We stood for what seemed liked minutes in that embrace. I thanked the Lord with the most sincerity I had ever had in my heart for this gift of reunion. I thanked him for overlooking all my awful, sinful ways and for giving me happiness again that I had not known in years.

I thought to myself that sometimes we run from the very thing we need. Something the good Lord tried to give us, and we were blind to see. I could see it now and in crystal clear form. I was going to hold on tight and savor every moment, every second, for the time we had left. I would no longer run from the thought of losing him. Love of this kind was more powerful than the fear of loss. Love never ended anyway. I understood that love could keep anyone alive, even at times of overwhelming grief. I leaned into Parker and held him as close as I could and still breathe. I whispered out loud, "Thank you, Lord. I am the most blessed person on earth."

A thought dawned on me suddenly, and I stepped away from him. "Constance! Oh, my Lord! She will shoot up to the moon when she hears about this! She will be the happiest woman in Augusta next to me! It is hard to believe this is all real, after all this time."

"My dear Celia, this is real, but you can kiss me again and make sure." I felt his embrace and his entire being surround me. It was a miracle. This was as close to heaven as one could find on this earth. While we embraced, I noticed the hawk was gliding in the sky over the valley below that was filled with the warm hues of sunset, then it turned and disappeared into the darkness of the trees. In that moment I wondered if the hawk was possibly a sign of sorts, a spirit maybe. How peculiar that the hawk had been near me all day. I wondered, was it Nathan's spirit?

I cleared that thought and pulled away from Parker and said, "Next Sunday I would like to attend church." Parker looked stunned, as if punched in the face, and leaned backwards in amazement of this statement.

"Celia, you are so unpredictable at times. I do love that about you though. Better make sure the reporter of the newspaper is there," he said. My face took on a puzzled look. "You know, in case you burst into flames when you walk through the door." Our laughter echoed down the hill and into the valley below. It all felt so right with Parker, as if time had never separated us.

"You know what? I think it is time we go inside and pretend we are already married," I said with a wink, as I reached for his hand. He gave me a little playful slap on my hind side and said, "I love the way you think, Miss Celia." Hand in hand and young at heart once more, we went in the house. We were full of love for each other with both our lives starting again.

Wrapped about each other, we both slept better than we had in years. But I awoke in the night with a jolt and a fearful thought. I needed to take care of

145

something right now before Parker woke. The brightness of the moon lit the room. I carefully eased out of bed and went to my desk in the living room and retrieved my journal. Then on I went to the hallway chest and found the other three journals I had saved from years before. In bare feet, I swiftly walked to the barn. I put all the journals in an empty feed sack and hid it under some straw bales. I was not going to mess this up again. I did not want Parker to find my journals and read about all my other liaisons. The first chance I got, I would burn all of them, except the pages about Parker. The only reason I had kept them at all was in the event that I might write my memoir. That seemed like such a pointless and imprudent idea, now that I had thought it in this moment.

Back to bed I went, spooning up to Parker. We both sighed in contentment. My heart felt loved. Life is complete now, I thought. So much better than I had ever hoped my last days would be. Why did it take me so long to get wiser about all this? Older and wiser was the saying. Hell, I had been old a long time already, and I am just now wised up. Guess I am a slow learner at times. Probably my stubborn nature, my daddy would say. If I died right now, I would most definitely die happy. It was blessing to feel this way so old in life and being not so far from life's end.

Wrapped around Parker, I dreamed of our wedding day. A wedding day was finally going to happen after all these years. I imagined that

Constance would want to bake the wedding cake. I pictured her standing there as my matron of honor, and Vernon as the best man. I envisioned the church decorated with sunflowers. They always reminded me of sunshine; sunshine on a stem. Yes, I would have a church full of sunshine on our wedding day. I breathed a long, contented sigh. I felt sleep coming over me.

I leaned over to kiss Parker. As I began to drift off to sleep again, I had one last thought that made me smile and chuckle. I could not wait to see the look of shock and disbelief on the face of Constance and the others at church next Sunday when I come sauntering in the door, arm in arm, with Parker. Seeing the shock on their faces that I had arrived to attend church services would be a *priceless* moment indeed. Hearing the announcement of my marriage, just might knock them all to the floor. And that would *unquestionably* be quite newsworthy.

Christine Bradfield

Discussion Questions

for

Book Groups

Celia talks about regret in chapter one. Do you agree or disagree with her ideas? And why?

Celia asks for divine intervention when presented with a stressful, troubling situation. Do you think that is common place? If so, why is that?

Parker refers to seeing Celia on the train as fate. Celia refers to events as divine intervention. Do you see these terms as the same, similar, or not alike at all? Have you ever judged a moment in your life as fate or divine intervention?

Why do you think that Celia didn't want Parker to see her looking for him in the train car window?

Celia expresses that she sometimes hated that she felt the need to care about others because it frequently put her in awkward and uncomfortable situations. Do you think this is true or not? And why? Do you think this is why sometimes people do not step up into help others?

Celia says if she had not been hurt by Clancy Jerdee, just prior to meeting Parker, she may not have pushed Parker away. What did you imagine Clancy had done to hurt her so deeply? What types of transgressions would you think would hurt someone so much?

Parker seems to have changed to the idea of divine intervention in the last chapter. Previously he called their meeting on the train fate. Do you think he has made a change in his thinking and beliefs? And if so, why do you think that?

Do you think the hawk was a spirit? Nathan's spirit? Do you know why the author might have chosen a hawk over another type of bird?

How would you describe Celia's internal journey? How do you think she has changed over the course of the book? Over the course of her life? If so, how do you imagine she will live life from now on, now that she has Parker?

We know what harsh things can happen in a person's life when they get older, but what good things would you imagine could happen to Celia and Parker once they are newlyweds?

About the Author

Christine Bradfield is a retired librarian who served her hometown library for over 26 years. Until a few years ago, she had never contemplated being a writer. A series of serendipitous events lead her to discover the joy of writing and in becoming an accidental author. She is pursuing writing with enthusiasm and delight, and she is self-publishing her works, for now.

Besides fiction, Christine has other writing interests that include nonfiction, poetry, short stories, and juvenile picture books. Her nonfiction book, *Two Kids and a Talking Crow: A True Story*, was published in October 2020. She is fascinated by the beautiful, heartbreaking, and humorous stories in everyday lives, and she desires to save as many of those as she can from being lost. She released her first juvenile picture book, *Millie's Boots*, a story of the special mother daughter bond, in November of 2021, along with her first book of poetry, *From Heart to Hand: Poetry of Life*. She is currently working on another title called, *The Horse Creek Boys: A Friendship of Misfits*, which she hopes to publish in 2022. Her published titles are also available for libraries to purchase through major library vendors such as Overdrive and Baker & Taylor.

Christine loves retirement and the time it allows her to discover and learn. When she reflects on how her life has unfolded, she believes everything and everyone during her library career has influenced, inspired, or taught her skills that has prepared her for this new venture. Libraries are awesome and are so necessary! Librarians rock and have the quiet power of a superhero! She will always be a library lover and supporter. She encourages everyone to get a library card and use its power of possibilities.